Praise

"The next Louis L'Amour."

— *USA Today* Best-Selling Author Roseanne
Bittner on Peter Brandvold

*"B.N. Rundell is the Louis L'Amour of our generation. Each
book is a page turner that you can't put down."*

— Amazon Review

"A good solid fist-slinging, gunslinging read."

— William W. Johnstone on L.J. Martin's
Stranahan

"Nesbitt is a true artist."

— *Western American Literature*

*"Chris Mullen's writing is sharp and action packed. His
talent and enthusiasm are enviable."*

— Chris Enss, *New York Times* best-selling
author

*"Ken Pratt knows how to make readers feel like...they are
part of the action."*

— Amazon Review

Ridin' with the Pack

Also by the Authors

Yakima Henry Western Series

Peter Brandvold

McCain Chronicles

B.N. Rundell

Two Thousand Grueling Miles Series

L.J. Martin

West of Dancing Rock & Other Western Stories

John D. Nesbitt

Rowdy Series

Chris Mullen

Matt Bannister Series

Ken Pratt

The Wyoming Chronicles

W. Micheal Gear

Ridin' with the Pack

A Western Short Story Collection

Peter Brandvold   B.N. Rundell   L.J. Martin
John D. Nesbitt   Chris Mullen   Ken Pratt
W. Micheal Gear

Edited by
Jake Bray

WOLFPACK
PUBLISHING
— EST 2013 —

Ridin' with the Pack: A Western Short Story Collection
Paperback Edition
Copyright © 2023 Jake Bray and the Individual Authors:
Peter Brandvold; B.N. Rundell; L.J. Martin; John D. Nesbitt; Chris Mullen;
Ken Pratt; W. Micheal Gear

Wolfpack Publishing
701 S. Howard Ave. 106-324
Tampa, Florida 33609

wolfpackpublishing.com

Paperback ISBN 978-1-63977-192-9
eBook ISBN 978-1-63977-191-2
LCCN 2023951025

Foreword

Dear Readers,

Welcome to our anthology of Western fiction, *Ridin' with the Pack*. This book is a testament to the timeless allure of the Western narrative, featuring stories from some of the finest authors in the genre. It's an honor to present these tales, which weave together the past and present of the American West, showcasing the talents of both legendary and emerging writers.

Western fiction holds a special place in our hearts. It embodies the spirit of adventure, the resilience of the human spirit, and a deep connection to the vast, rugged landscapes that define the American West. This anthology is a celebration of that spirit, bringing together stories that resonate with authenticity, grit, and an unyielding sense of adventure.

In these pages, you'll find an array of characters and land-scapes. From the stoic determination of man out for revenge for the deaths of his family, to the struggles of a family locked in an epic battle to save their land, home, and heritage—each story offers a unique glimpse into the heart of the West. These narratives showcase the genre's classic themes—courage, honor, and justice—while also exploring new frontiers in Western storytelling.

At Wolfpack Publishing, we're committed to honoring the rich legacy of Western fiction while also fostering its growth. This anthology represents that commitment, blending the voices of established masters with the fresh perspectives of new writers. Each author contributes not just a story, but a piece of the larger narrative that defines our understanding of the Western experience.

I extend a heartfelt thank you to our authors, whose talent and dedication make this collection possible. Their stories are a reminder of why we fell in love with Western fiction in the first place. They carry the torch of the great Western writers, illuminating the path for future generations.

Looking ahead, I want to reach out to the storytellers among you who share our passion for the West. If you have a tale that captures the essence of the Western spirit, we at Wolfpack Publishing would be honored to consider it for next year's anthology. This is more than an invitation—it's a call to join us in celebrating and continuing the rich tradition of Western storytelling.

I invite you to delve into this anthology and embark on a journey through the heart of the American West. These stories are a tribute to the enduring legacy of the Western spirit, a spirit that continues to inspire and move us. So, saddle up and join us on this adventure. The trail awaits!

Warm regards,

Jake Bray
Editor
President, Wolfpack Publishing

Ridin' with the Pack

Hair of the Dog

Peter Brandvold

Hair of the Dog

LUKE RADEK GRABBED THE DEAD MAN BY A HANDFUL OF HAIR and yanked him down off the horse on which the bounty hunter had packed the outlaw's bloating carcass into Ute Springs, Colorado Territory.

"Good Lord, man!" exclaimed the little, older-than-the-hills town lawman Marshal H. W. "Cimarron" Cody, taking one step straight back from the bloating bag of bones and closing his arm across his nose and mustache-mantled mouth. "How long you been trailing this passel of rotten nastiness?"

The handsome, blond Radek laughed. "What's the matter, Marshal? You gone soft in your old age? Why, you act like a sissified dandy that never saw a cadaver before!"

"Oh, I seen plenty, young feller," said Cimarron Cody. "Believe me—*plenty*! Mescins, Injuns, bluebellies, graybacks. But never by *choice*! An' I hate smellin' 'em even more!"

Again, the younger man—younger by a good forty years than Cody, who had to be pushing seventy—twirled his pearl-handled .45 Colt Peacemaker on his gloved, right index finger and laughed. "I don't smell 'em anymore. I guess I've become in...in...what's the word I'm lookin' for? Dated a

schoolteacher once, and I knew the word but for the life
of me—"

"Manured to it," said Cody. "That's the word."

"You sure?"

"No, but it's right fittin'. Good Lord, man!" the small-
town lawman said with his arm over his nose.

"Ah, hell, I only been trailin' ol' Teagarden here for…"

The tall, chisel-featured, duster-clad Radek pouched the
stylish hogleg and cast his brown-eyed gaze beyond a near
grassy beaver meadow toward the San Juan Mountains rising
like a giant, purple sawblade in the west. "Let me see," said
the bounty hunter, squinting at the sky and counting in his
head. "Nigh on five days now, I'd say. Yeah, yeah. Must be
five. Fellas in my line of work, who work for no one but
themselves"—he proudly thumped himself in the chest—
"lose track of time now an' then, don't ya know?"

At thirty-four, Radek was one of the most successful
bounty hunters on the western frontier. He knew it, and that
self-confidence—some might call it arrogance—glittered in
his eyes. He'd grown up in the East, but he hadn't been born
with any silver spoon in his mouth. He'd made his way west
on his own, taught himself to shoot on his own.

To kill on his own…

"Stinks to high heaven!" intoned Cody. "Just had my
twice-yearly bath yesterday mornin'. Think I'm gonna take
me another'n tonight…get the stench off. Hate to waste the
water, but…"

"Complain, complain, complain," Radek said. "When I
bring in only the heads in gunnysacks—complain, complain,
complain! When I bring in the whole damn carcass, stem to
stern—complain, complain, complain!" He toed the corpse
whose large, pale, puffy face glared up at the two men staring
down at him. "Is he not ugly as sin? That's what I hate worse
than the stench. Ugly! I'll be glad to not have to look at Henry
W. "Hog" Teagarden's ugly countenance ever again!"

The younger man laughed again, wagged his head, and kicked Teagarden's ribs, making the big body rock to each side.

"Tell you what, Marshal—why don't you fetch me the bounty for this big, ugly slab of stage-robbin' meat, an' I'll have me a plate of vittles and a few mouthfuls of labeled bourbon, if there is such a thing as a labeled bottle in this neck of the woods. Been cravin' some good Tennessee bug juice for days now; I ran out just north of Mesilla. Been a long, dry ride. But that's all right. I like to stay alert. Never know when some varmint's gonna try to backshoot me, steal my prize."

He looked down at the dead man, staring up at him from sightless, hazel eyes set deep in bloated, bluish-pale sockets.

Cody said, "I'll cable the federals in Denver for a promissory note so I can get repaid then head over to the bank. Hope ol' Fiedler has a thousand greenbacks layin' around or you're out o' luck. Have to hang around for a payout straight from the feds themselves. Meantime, you can do a lot worse than the busthead an' vittles ol' Sanchez slings at the Blind Coyote."

The lawman, his head looking unnaturally small under the large, gray, sugarloaf sombrero he wore, jerked his chin to indicate the saloon sitting on the other side of the street from his humble jailhouse constructed from logs cut from the surrounding, forested ridges and which composed most of the other dwellings scattered around the canyon Ute Springs had been built in. There were three bullet holes in the sign stretching into the street from the lawman's office reading TOWN MARSHAL. A fat tabby cat was asleep on a rail of the rickety porch, near the bloody remains of a dead rat.

The old lawman turned to amble off in his bandy-legged fashion toward the Western Union office. Western Union and the Blind Coyote, the saloon Cody had indicated, appeared two of the only six or seven businesses remaining open in Ute Springs, the gold having been plundered from the surrounding streams and ridges years ago. The steep, pine- and fir-carpeted peaks surrounding the town lent the breeze a winy tang. The ridges surrounded what was left of the town, rather. The large, gaudy, albeit badly faded sign over the pine branch ramada fronting the Blind Coyote bespoke more pros- perous and optimistic times here in Ute Springs.

The wild, old times...

Now the only traffic was a lone ranch wagon clattering down the street, manned by an old cowpuncher in a blue plaid shirt with patched elbows and faded denims with patched knees. He appeared half-asleep on the driver's seat of the rocking buckboard. He muttered something Radek could hear then turned the brindle mule in the traces toward the two-story dry goods store slumped under its rusted tin roof, on the same side of the street as Cimarron's jailhouse and a half block farther south along the broad, forlorn-looking main street, with another badly faded sign called Bighorn Avenue.

Radek tied his gelding to a hitchrack fronting the Blind Coyote and shucked his prized Winchester repeater, which he'd had custom made by a gunsmith in Denver and which boasted a pistol handle and a sliding rear sight for long-range work, from its black leather scabbard. He set the long gun on his shoulder, stepped under the arbor, crossed the small stoop, and pushed through the Blind Coyote's swing doors.

As was his custom, for man hunters worth their salt made enemies, he stepped to one side so the doorway wouldn't outline him, making him an easy target.

The place was empty.

Still, the smell of man sweat mingled with the stench of stale whiskey, sawdust, and cheap perfume.

The bar lay to Radek's left.

He went over to the five long pine planks stretched across three iron-banded beer kegs and ordered a beer and a shot of whiskey from the big, half-breed bartender, the sex of whom the bounty man could not determine. There appeared two lumps behind the apron's loose wool shirt, but whether they were female lumps or male lumps Radek couldn't tell. Long, nearly coal-black hair framed the man or woman's long, flat, vaguely, bizarrely feminine face and molasses-dark eyes.

"You got any liquor with a label on it?" Radek asked, opening and closing his hand around the neck of the rifle resting on his shoulder.

The apron gave a raking grunt and a murmured response that Radek could not understand as he or she filled a shot glass from an unlabeled bottle and filled a mug from a spout poking up out of a beer keg before promptly disappearing through a curtained doorway behind the bar. Radek could hear a definite woman's voice back there, but she spoke too quietly for the bounty hunter to make out what she was saying.

Radek picked up his frothy beer mug and whiskey shot, which he winced at, knowing the quality of the liquor served this far off the beaten track. He moseyed over to a table, kicked out a chair, slacked into it, and removed his gloves and crisp, cream Stetson. He set both along with the rifle on the table.

He leaned back and lazily built a cigarette. He fired a match on his thumbnail, lit the quirley, waved out the match, and dropped it on the sawdust-covered floor. The sawdust could not conceal several bullet holes in the ancient wood, he absently noticed. Nor the dark-brown patches that could only be bloodstains. Some older than others.

Yes, Ute Springs had stomped with its tail up at one time.

Now it was as tame as a house cat.

Now it was taking that long, slow plunge back into the earth from which it had come. The way of the world, Radek silently mused. But then, it was men like him who'd made it that way. He himself had thrown a hand in on getting the frontier West on its leash—of cleaning out the old salts, the roughshod warriors from the wild, old times...Of turning the wild open towns into ghost towns.

Of course, it helped that the gold and silver had pinched out of the creeks and streams surrounding Ute Springs and so many other boomtowns just like it.

But Luke Radek and others like him had had a hand in it, all right.

He sipped the rotgut whiskey, congratulating himself on his forbearance, for not complaining as some would do. He sipped the beer, as well. It was only marginally better than the tarantula juice. Slowly, thoughtfully, he smoked the quirley, watching the late-day shadows stretch out from the western ridges, filling the canyon with an early dusk. The westering sun turned softer, gentler, easier on the eyes where it hung between craggy ridges silhouetted against it.

A cool breeze gentled in over the batwings, touched with the smell of stone and forest loam and pine needles from the higher reaches where Ute warriors once hunted bighorn sheep and the topknots of mountain men and fur trappers, where army deserters and outlaws once fled to cool their heels.

The wild, old times...

Radek had to draw himself a second beer and splash a second shot of what passed for whiskey in these parts into his glass, as the male or female apron did not heed his summons. He smelled spicy chili emanating from the back room, however. It evoked hunger pangs in the bounty hunter. He was on his way back to his table when Cimarron Cody appeared, pushing through the batwings, a grin on his gray-mustached face that, while deeply age-lined, the lines encrusted with ancient dirt and grime, looked boy-sized and none too vaguely cadaverous under the frayed brim of his old sombrero.

"You're in luck!"

He waved a manila envelope in his gnarled, brown right hand, cackling.

He ambled over to Radek's table, saying, "Ol' Fiedler just happened to have a thousand notes layin' around, though he had to hunt for it. Made him mad, it did. That was his last thousand, the bank's own money. Woke him from a nap with his favorite doxie—Miss Carlene. Last workin' girl in town!"

The old marshal chuckled and slapped the envelope down on the table fronting Radek.

The bounty hunter opened it, counted the bills, raised his shot glass in salute to the marshal of Ute Springs, and tossed back the entire shot, sucking a sharp breath through gritted teeth. "Ah...the Who-Hit-John. That'll hit him *hard*!"

He chuckled, proud of his own good nature.

Cody ambled around behind the bar, tossed a coin into a tin can, and came back with his own shot of whiskey. "Mind if I join you? The boy who works for the undertaker should be along in a minute, take that stinky mess off your hands."

Radek kicked out a chair. "Sit down, Marsh..."

He let his voice trail off. Frowning, he turned toward the batwings. Through a dirty, warped window to the right of the swing doors he saw a horseback rider ride past the Blind Coyote, a shaggy, black-and-white collie dog trotting along beside him, a long, dead but still-writhing rattlesnake hanging from the dog's jaws. The rider led a paint horse outfitted with canvas panniers by a hackamore rope.

Cody followed the bounty hunter's gaze and chuckled. He wagged his head, sipped his whiskey. Radek was mildly curious about the rider and the dog but then the old, bearded mountain salt and his two horses and his dog disappeared, likely heading for the mercantile to lay in supplies for the long mountain winter ahead. Such men once honeycombed the high reaches of the west. These days, near the turn of the century, they were a dying breed.

Radek and Cimarron Cody spoke in desultory tones for a

time but then the old, bearded rider on a stout buckskin trailing the pack horse, its paniers now bulging, the dog following with half the snake hanging from its jaws, appeared again. This time they were angling toward the Blind Coyote.

Radek gazed through the window as the old mountain salt swung down from the saddle of his short, stocky buckskin—a mountain horse, for sure—slipped the cinch and bit, and tossed the reins over the hitchrack. "Who's that?"

"Never mind about him," Cody said. "Regular here. *Ir*regular here, I should say. But ol' Sanchez always seems to know when he's comin' for supplies and to sorta see the elephant, you might say. Thus, the chili you smell."

The newcomer turned from the hitchrack to glance at the dead man on the ground by the packhorse then turned again to stare through the window.

He looked even older close up. Old and stooped with a thick tangle of gray beard, skin almost as dark as ol' Sanchez's, whom Radek had now determined was male. The newcomer wore a buckskin tunic, suspenders, and baggy canvas trousers. A shell belt with a soft brown holster encircled his lean waist. A paunch hung down over the buckle.

The belt was low slung, the holster bristling with an old-model, brass-framed, cap-and-ball revolver. The hat on his wizened, blue-eyed head was an age- and weather-battered gray Confederate campaigner with a few tassels of gilt braiding remaining, trimming the crown.

Radek's heart quickened. He stared at the holstered hogleg. He'd bet aces to eights it was an old Civil War model, Confederate-made Griswold & Gunnison, manufactured in Georgia and fashioned after the 1851 Navy Colt.

The former grayback spat a long wad of chaw to one side, wiped his mouth with the back of his gloved right hand, then turned away from the window.

Presently, boots thudded on the boardwalk fronting the saloon. The newcomer pushed through the batwings, the dog, the snake still dangling from its jaws, still writhing slowly, grotesquely, close on his heels.

The old-timer's keen blue eyes swept the room, landed for a brief second on Radek, and a fleeting smile tugged at his mouth corners. He clomped over to the bar, spurs chinging. He reached the worn planks into which many initials and ranch brands had been carved over the years just as the half-breed, Sanchez, emerged from the back room, not so much walking as sashaying on thick hips, a loosely rolled, cornhusk cigarette dangling from between his thick lips.

"Wilbur, you old *pendejo*," the barman said in his strangely feminine, nasal voice, heavily Spanish accented, ashes dripping from the end of his quirley. "I woke up this mornin' at the crack of dawn, took a look outside, an' I said to myself, 'Eduardo, this looks like a day Wilbur an' Old Shep are gonna come down out o' them mountains an' pay you a visit. You better get some chili on the stove!"

He slapped a thick, pale hand onto the bar. "Am I not like one o' them hoo-doo witches, *o no lo soy*?" Or am I not?

The newcomer laughed a raking laugh, drew a deep breath into his bony chest and said something that to Radek's ears sounded like perfect Spanish. He looked down at the collie dog lying at his feet. The dog was hungrily devouring the snake, holding its still-writhing body down with his paws, ripping, tearing, and swallowing large mouthfuls.

His eyes riveted on the back of the newcomer; the bounty hunter's heart quickened.

Wilbur...

He could hardly catch his breath.

He had that tight feeling in his chest and throat a man gets when he's confronted by something wild. Primitive. Primeval.

A silver-tipped grizzly, say. A white buffalo. A black fox. The ghost of an Apache warrior who'd once ridden with Cochise, Victorio, or Mangas Coloradas.

It was the kind of feeling a man gets when he's confronted by a ghost, though Radek had to admit he really didn't know. He'd never been confronted by a ghost before. Until now…

A ghost with a thirty-five-hundred-dollar bounty on his head. That amount had been twice as high just after the war.

A train-robbing old Confederate who'd headed west just after the War Between the States, after killing his wife and his best friend whom he'd found in bed together the same day he'd come home to resume his old life, the one he'd had before the War of Northern Aggression. The humble, quiet life of a farmer.

Shot them both dead, as Radek recalled hearing the old story. The family of the wife, prominent Southerners, had put a bounty on his head, one that had never been collected though it was said the man's own son, a deputy United States marshal, had tried to avenge his mother's murder. He'd ridden into this wild country only a year ago last winter and was never seen or heard from again.

Wilbur Calhoun.

That was the name!

As famous at one time as his fellow bushwhackers Jesse and Frank James and their cousin, Cole Younger.

Sometime in the seventies, just after he and his gang, most of whom were now dead or in prison, had planned and executed an especially lucrative train robbery, striking the Central Pacific as they had so many times before.

Wilbur Calhoun.

Sure enough.

Before Radek's very eyes…

The old bushwhacker slapped the bar and railed off another string of perfect Spanish, adding in what Radek assumed was the name of the dog, Old Shep. Radek had picked up some Spanish over the years. Calhoun spoke too rapidly for the bounty hunter to keep up, but he picked out enough to know the old outlaw wanted a bottle of busthead and a bowl of chili.

A shot first, then more later, with the chili.

He'd stable his horses and then he'd be back...to stay the night—he pointed at the ceiling—in a room upstairs.

He threw back the whiskey, slammed the glass down on the bar, raised his old campaigner to rake a big hand through his thick, silver hair that hung to his shoulders. He told the dog to stay and finish his meal. He'd be back.

Wilbur Calhoun would be back.

The white buffalo would return.

He left.

Warm blood coursed eagerly through the bounty hunter's veins. The bounty on Calhoun's head might not be worth much these days. But he had a reputation, notoriety. Whoever killed him would become part of his story, his legend.

Radek snapped his fingers at the barman and pointed at his glass.

He'd be here awhile.

WHEN WILBUR CALHOUN returned to the saloon, the collie, who had finished the snake in his owner's absence, leaving only the sawdusted head lying staring blankly beside a spittoon, thumped his tail happily.

The half-breed barman, Sanchez, set a bottle and a bowl of stew on the bar, and Calhoun dug in hungrily. Cimarron Cody had finished his whiskey and retreated to his jailhouse to finish the paperwork he grouchingly attributed to Radek and to "close up shop for the night."

Since Radek had decided to spend the night in the saloon, close to his quarry, waiting for the opportunity to take down the old Confederate outlaw, he left to stable his horses in the only livery barn left in town. The big, ugly, fittingly nicknamed "Hog" Teagarden had been hauled away for planting. Radek returned to the Blind Coyote when there was only a little light left in the sky between the velvet-black western ridges beyond the grassy beaver meadow, and the first stars were kindling in the east.

As he pushed through the batwings, he saw Calhoun sitting at a table on the far side of a potbelly stove from the table at which the bounty hunter and Cody had been sitting previously. Cody had returned to join the man, as had the old cowpuncher whom Radek had seen pulling his buckboard up to the mercantile when the bounty hunter had first ridden into Ute Springs with his grisly cargo. Sanchez was there, as well, kicked back in a chair that appeared as though it could barely hold him. He was smoking and conversing in jovial tones of joint reminiscence, sometimes in English, sometimes in Spanish, all four men often breaking into raucous laughter, slapping their hands and clinking their glasses together in salute.

Since Sanchez seemed to be ignoring him, Radek helped himself to whiskey at the bar, finally deciding that since he was spending the night, he might as well buy a bottle though he feared the coffin varnish might burn a hole through his belly and leave his insides pouring onto the floor at his feet.

The festivities on the other side of the potbelly stove, in which Sanchez had built a fire to stave off the mountain night's customary chill, continued for the next hour. The shaggy collie lay curled in contented sleep, chin resting on his paws, at Calhoun's feet. Radek had to admit to feeling a little left out. A time or two, he almost went over and asked if he could join the four old frontiersmen but decided it might give Calhoun the advantage in some way, and that he wouldn't be welcome, anyway, so he remained at his own table with his own bottle of forty-rod.

He kept his own council, reminding him of his superiority over the four old salts. They were part of a bygone era, one which Radek himself had helped close the book on. The book was not yet entirely closed, however. There was still Wilbur Calhoun, whom the bounty hunter saw as sort of the last outlaw. One he would take down.

And then the book on that era would, indeed, be closed.

And he'd be the one who'd finally closed it.

As the night wore on and the conversation on the far side of the room from the bounty hunter grew more and more raucous, Radek heard the thuds of approaching horses. One of the horses whinnied. If the four old salts heard the newcomers, they didn't let on. Calhoun and the old cowpuncher, whom Radek had heard called Jube, probably short for Jubal, were listening intently to what sounded like a tirade being delivered by Sanchez. Something about being cheated by a former business partner who had ruined the half-breed financially and run off with his wife.

Radek vaguely understood that the business associate had come to a bad end. Sanchez punctuated his story with an angry, high-pitched growl, a show of large, rotten, brown teeth, and a sweep of his crooked right index finger across his throat.

The other three men laughed.

Sanchez slapped the table.

They were still laughing as two men clad in dusty trail gear entered the saloon. Both looked weary, hungry, and thirsty. Sanchez got up to serve them whiskey and chili and then, when both men were standing at the bar, hunkered over their drinks and chili, ragged hats on the bar beside them, the half-breed returned to the table of friendly palaver. He brought a beef bone for Old Shep, who dug into the meaty bone with the same relish as he had the snake.

The dog growled, snarled, whined, yipped, ripped, and tore, holding the bone down with one paw. He seemed to be pretending the bone were some varmint he'd half killed, like the snake, and was endeavoring to kill the other half. Both newcomers in shaggy trail gear regarded the dog distaste-fully over their shoulders as they ate and sipped their drinks.

Radek saw the disgust and anger in them grow.

Meanwhile, the four old salts continued to palaver and swill the rotgut though they spoke over each other so much it was hard for Radek to get a handle on their stories. They certainly seemed to be enjoying them, though. Four old relics. Dead men sitting there with their wild old times. They just didn't know it yet. Or maybe they did but ignored it, prefer-ring to believe the wild old times were better days.

That was the way of foolish old men.

All four should be locked up for some of the things they'd confessed to over the past couple of hours.

Finally, the drover standing to the right of the other one, the shorter of the pair and who had curly, red-brown hair and a fat, round, boyish face, pulled the Schofield .44 from the holster on his right thigh. He turned to the dog still growling and gnawing on the leg bone.

"That dog is pure nasty! Why, he done upset our appetites!"

The four old salts fell silent. They looked up at the obvious drifter.

Old Shep was looking at him, too, raising his hackles, showing his teeth, growling.

"Look at him—he ain't fit fer civilized company. What that cur needs is a *bullet*, and I aim to give him one!"

He raised the Schofield and aimed it at angle down at the growling dog.

A gun blasted once, twice, three times.

Only it wasn't Curly's gun that had spoken.

Radek's mind whirled at the sudden cacophony, at the screams of the two men at the bar. After Curly had taken the first bullet, the other, taller drifter had whipped around, reaching for his own holstered revolver. The second round had taken him in the chest. The third one had finished Curly and driven him to the floor.

There was one more loud explosion, and the taller gent screamed again, turned to the bar. He dug his fingers into the edge of it, trying to hold himself up. But they slid down over the edge, and he dropped to lie flat on his back on the sawdusted floor.

Radek looked at the old salts' table.

Jube and Sanchez were laughing through their teeth as Wilbur Calhoun, who'd been sitting with his back to the bar, turned forward in his chair and slid the old Griswold & Gunnison back into the holster tied low on his thigh.

Old Shep got up, walked over to the dead men, and lifted his leg on Curly. He trotted back to his bone, flopped down on it as though it were still-living prey, and resumed his toil, growling, snarling, ripping, and tearing...

———

RADEK WENT to bed long before the four old frontiersmen did.

He lay awake, fully clothed on the lumpy bed, hands entwined behind his head, listening to the four men roaring and clinking glasses and slapping their table in the drinking hall below. He couldn't have slept with such a commotion if he'd wanted to. He didn't want to. Despite himself, he found himself enjoying what he could understand of the stories being relayed in both English and Spanish below.

He was so trail tired that he found himself nodding off, taking short snoozes, before being awakened by another blast of ribald laughter.

Finally, the roaring dwindled.

The old salts raked their chairs back, yawning, speaking a few last words, enjoying a few last remnants of revelry, and then boots thudded and spurs rang as they went their own separate ways. Jube the cowpuncher and Cimarron Cody left the saloon, batwings clattering, and Wilbur Calhoun loudly climbed the stairs one loud clomp at a time. Radek knew it was Calhoun. The bounty hunter could hear the clicks of the dog's nails on the stairs. By now, Radek could identify the old man's voice as he spoke softly to the dog. He yawned as he tramped a little unsteadily along the hall, spurs ringing.

As he approached Radek's door, the bounty hunter closed his hand around the grips of his .45 still strapped around his waist. He released the keeper thong from over the hammer and began to ease the gun from the holster.

How easy it would be to take ol' Calhoun down now...

He was drunk and off guard.

The loud footsteps died abruptly just outside Radek's door.

Radek pricked his ears. He could hear Calhoun's raspy breathing out there in the hall on the other side of the bounty hunter's door. The dog panted.

Radek's blood quickened. He tightened his grip on his gun handle.

But then the footsteps resumed—of both man and dog—and dwindled off down the hall, Calhoun saying, "Come on, Shep. You can warm my cold old feet tonight." A doorknob squawked as it turned, a door opened, the hinges squawking, as well. The door closed with a thump. Bed springs creaked as a bed accepted the old-timer's drunken, potbellied, slump-shouldered body.

Almost instantly, loud snoring issued from two or three doors down the hall.

Radek removed his hand from the .45.

He could easily slip out of his room and shoot the old outlaw and his mangy cur through the door of his room. The bounty would be his. But that wasn't Radek's way. No, when he took down Calhoun, he'd take him down in the old man's stomping grounds, in the high-and-rocky. On the man's own terms.

Radek wanted no unfair advantage. He wanted to take his prized quarry down fairly. He'd outsmart him fairly. Kill him fairly.

He'd accept the money on Calhoun's head knowing that it was clean, fair money. There would be many stories told about the encounter—of the younger, modern man getting the drop on the older, more experienced one. That would be the stuff of legend, just as old Calhoun was now the subject of tales of the wild old times told around saloons throughout the West.

Of course, Radek's taking down Calhoun still wouldn't be fair.

Radek had the advantage over the older man because the bounty hunter was younger and stronger. Faster, too. With better vision and hearing.

No, it wouldn't really be fair. It couldn't be. Radek was in his prime. Still, the stories would be told, Radek's name would be mentioned in magazines and history books read by generations to come.

The bounty hunter smiled. Yawned. Slept.

───────

RADEK WAS DOWNSTAIRS BY SUNUP, eating two fried eggs over a bowl of chili and washing the savory concoction down with deep drafts of beer.

He was content.

Not just content. He was celebrating. Inwardly, at least. Inwardly, he was smiling.

He shaped a stone-faced expression when he heard boots and paws on the stairs. He turned to see his elderly quarry, Wilbur Calhoun, clomping down the steps. Calhoun moved slowly, carefully, steadying himself with one hand on the rail, which creaked against his uncertain descent. The old train robber looked especially haggard, his craggy, bearded face drawn, eyes red-rimmed and washed out.

The dog following him down was old too, with gray in his snout, but he looked much more ready to face the day of rabbit chasing and snake killing. His tail was up and his eyes were clear. He was panting, damn near smiling, if curs could smile. Radek knew they couldn't.

Calhoun smiled sheepishly when he saw Sanchez standing behind the bar, looking no better for last night's wear and tear than Calhoun did. The barman drew his mouth corners down, wagged his head, and set an unlabeled bottle on the bar with aplomb.

"A little hair of the dog, amigo?" he called in his oddly feminine voice.

"Best medicine for a hangover I know of," Calhoun said, striding toward the bar, catching his boots on chair legs. Old Shep was close on his heels. The old outlaw slapped his hand down on the bar and said, "And a beer and an egg for breakfast. Fer both me an' Shep. Then we gotta hit the trail, don't ya know? Make sure no squatters have taken over our cabin! Done shot two last week when we come back from checkin' our trot lines. Ain't that right, Shep?"

The old dog gave a bark in response then lay down at its owner's feet, staring toward the window, likely on the scout for something more rib-sticking than beer and eggs. The whiskey, beer, and egg seemed to suit Calhoun just fine, however. Palavering in a desultory way with the big bartender, he drank down a third of the beer, tossed in the shot, and sipped the beer and the whiskey for only a few minutes before knocking back the egg, slapping his hand down on the bar, and saying, *"Hasta la próxima, amigo. ¡Recuerda mantener tu pene mojado, un dedo en el gatillo y un ojo en tu rastro!"*

He and Sanchez roared, shook hands, and then Calhoun planted his faded gray campaigner on his head. Man and dog strode out through the batwings and into the buttery light of the Colorado mountain morning. A half hour later, hooves drummed. A dog barked. The drumming of two horses dwindled into the distance as the old train robber and his panting dog and a winter's worth of supplies retreated toward their mountain hideaway.

A place few men, if any, knew the location of. Radek would never know it, either. He didn't intend for the old outlaw to get that far.

He took his time with his breakfast, not wanting his intentions to be suspected. Twenty minutes after Calhoun had left, he finished his beer, wiped his mouth, yawned, set his hat on his head, and rose from his chair. He dropped coins on the table, smiled and waved at the apron, who stood staring at him dully—suspiciously?—from behind the bar, then left to saddle his own two horses.

———

"WELL, I'LL BE DAMNED," the bounty hunter said quietly to himself later that evening, after he'd been trailing Calhoun from a good distance all day. "He must've gone addlepated in his old age!"

Radek adjusted the focus on his field glasses. He stared through them again, pulled them down, blinked his eyes as though to clear them, then raised the glasses once more.

"Sure enough," he muttered just above a wheeze. "He's layin' out there by a big fire. Has a big fire…a man whose been hunted for as many years as he has. Sure enough—has to be. He's gone soft in his thinker box!"

Could be a trap, he warned himself.

But he didn't think so.

Calhoun lay in his bedroll, leaned back against his saddle propped against a tree, hat brim pulled low over his eyes. It was a cold night. He had his arms crossed under the blankets.

His feet stuck out from the end of the bedroll, within only a few inches of the orange flames dancing inside the fire ring.

From where he hunkered low on a shallow ridge, surrounded by pines and firs, again the bounty hunter swept the camp below with his gaze. He'd thought it might be a ruse, and when he stole down there and entered the old outlaw's camp, he'd find the bedroll filled only with pine limbs, and he'd get a bullet in his back for his stupidity.

But Radek was not a stupid man.

And this wasn't his first rodeo.

"Been living alone with just the dog," he said to himself now, feeling his lips stretch away from his teeth with a coyote grin. "Gone soft in his thinker box. Gone careless. Maybe thinks the world has forgotten about him."

Radek shook his head.

"Not me. Not Luke Radek."

Again, he smiled. Lowering the glasses, he shook his head. "No...no...no. Not me."

He looked for the dog. Couldn't see him. Probably off hunting rabbits. He was an old cur, but he was a hunter. Not long for this world, either, if he came back to camp before Radek wanted him to. Calhoun's horses were picketed in the trees and brush on the other side of the camp. Radek made sure he'd positioned himself downwind from the mount, whose senses were likely a whole lot keener than its rider's.

He got up and returned the binoculars to his saddlebags. Wielding his Winchester, wearing a fleece-lined coat against the mountain chill, he pulled his hat brim down and stole down and around the shoulder of the slope. The ridge pulled away on his left and when Radek moved out from behind a small pine, the fire came into clear view, sparks rising from the flames and going out a few feet up in the night-black sky above the camp. In view now, as well, was the old man lying on the other side of the fire from the bounty hunter, flat out, not a care in the world. Radek could even hear him snoring that loud, grating snore he had heard in the saloon last night and which had woken him often, grinding his teeth in annoyance.

It had made him want to put a bullet in him then and there and get it over with.

Once on the floor of the hollow Calhoun had pitched his camp in, Radek slowed his pace. He'd removed his spurs, and he moved silently through the long grass, weaving around cedar clumps and pines. He prided himself on how quietly he could move. As quiet as an Apache. Slow as a near-frozen mountain stream though he could be lightning quick when he needed to be.

Taking one slow step at a time, he watched the fire grow larger before him, casting light and umber shadows around the camp. The snores grew louder. He could see the old man's swollen feet. Pale as a dead man's, bulging here and there with bunions and corns. The nails thick and yellow as clamshells.

He was within ten feet of the camp now, quartering around the fire to his right, Calhoun's left. You always came up on a man from the opposite side of his gun side. Last night in the saloon, he'd seen that the old bank robber was right-handed. Not much got past Luke Radek.

He smiled, ran the tip of his tongue along the underside of his upper lip, moistening it. He looked around again for the dog. No sign of the motley beast. Good.

He was within six feet of the snoring Calhoun.

Five...four...three...

He stopped. Extending the Winchester straight out in his right hand, he crouched, grabbed an edge of the old killer's blankets, and jerked them down and away, tossing them toward the fire. He swiped the hat off the old bank robber's head with the back of his left hand...

And gazed down in hang-jawed shock.

His heart raced and his knees shook in horror as he stared

not at the bearded, sun-seasoned countenance of Wilbur Calhoun but at the bloated, pale-blue, ugly countenance of Henry W. "Hog" Teagarden who stared back at him with an enraged, hazel-eyed, death-mask grimace!

The snoring stopped.

Calhoun poked his head out from behind the tree flanking the dead man.

He poked his Winchester '73 repeater out from behind the tree, as well. Firelight glinted in the bluing.

He grinned inside his tangled beard, blue eyes twinkling mischievously.

"Well, if you don't beat a hen a'flyin'!" he cackled.

Radek stood frozen. Shock had turned him to stone.

"Why you," he said, horrified by his mistake and finding no other words to utter. "Why you..."

"Damn fool," Calhoun said, mildly. "This ain't this ol' boy's first rodeo, you cork-headed tinhorn!"

Radek just stared at him. His heart hammered his breastbone.

"What?" he finally managed to say. "What..."

"Am I gonna do now?" The smile broadened inside the beard.

"Y-yeah," Radek heard himself say, voice brittle. "Yeah."

"Wouldn't be polite not to offer a little hair o' the dog—now, would it?" Calhoun glanced behind the bounty hunter. "Shep!"

Radek whipped around.

Before him was a large black-and-white blur and two flashing, dark-brown eyes growing larger and larger as the dog came running and snarling around the fire to leap off his back legs and sink his well-honed teeth into the bounty hunter's throat.

Tugs

B.N. Rundell

Leaving

HE WAS A BEAR OF A MAN. A GOOD HAND TALLER THAN MOST
men and built in the shape and strength of a big oak barrel.
He weighed in at almost 18 stone and had a full head of thick
red hair and a face full of whiskers to match. With dark
brown eyes that accented his round red nose and a deep bass
voice, most men would step aside when they saw him
coming. But Red Pierce was a gentle giant, raised at his mother's knee as she taught him to read and write and know his
sums, he was educated past most of those in the entire village
that lay in the shadow of the tipples of the deep coal mine
that employed all the men. His mother had fallen to
consumption when he was still a lad and his father had
worked in the mine alongside his older brother, leaving Red
to take care of himself. But his size, after a growth spurt when
he turned twelve, was that of a full-grown man and his father
convinced him to follow in his footsteps and become a coal
miner.

Red had a hard time of it in the deep mines. Always
having to walk stooped over because of the low timbers, and
when he finished his shift and drew a deep breath of fresh air
and washed all the coal dust off, he determined to never

return. But return he did, time and again, until the last day when the roof fell in and trapped so many. Red had shouldered the last timber to allow several men to escape, but he lost his father and brother. When he ran from the cave-in, he knew he would never again go into the belly of the beast and with his savings from three years underground and the set aside for emergency money of his father and brother, he bought a dapple-gray Percheron horse that stood just over seventeen hands, weighed a bit more than a ton but had a personality that matched that of Red. With a sizable mule for a pack animal, he left Lansford, Pennsylvania, and the coal mines, bound for the far blue mountains called the Rockies. He wanted to be as far away from the black depths of the coal mines as possible and with the fresh air of the mountains to fill his lungs and rid them of the accumulated coal dust.

With a Sharps .50 in the scabbard under his right leg, and a Colt .44 Dragoon in a holster on his hip, he rode across Pennsylvania, caught a riverboat down the Allegheny to the Ohio, another boat to the Mississippi and another up the Mississippi and Missouri where he disembarked at Westport. He signed on with a freighter taking wagonloads of goods down the Santa Fe Trail to Bent's Fort where Red mounted his big grey, and pack mule in tow, started for the far blue mountains.

With the trader's fort behind him and the sun slowly rising to warm his back, Red rocked in his saddle, enjoying the feel of the horse beneath him, nothing before him but the distant mountains, and no living soul within sight anywhere. He let a slow grin paint his face and part his whiskers, a newfound sparkle in his eye as he cocked his head to the side and let out a deep belly laugh. It had been a long time since he had enough carefree attitude to elicit a laugh, but this vast land and its unlimited freedom was a new thing to be enjoyed. He chuckled as he let his eyes rove from south to north and back again. On his left, the meandering Arkansas

River chuckled through the cottonwoods and willows. To his right, scattered juniper and piñon freckled the plains that stretched further than eye could see, land that was carpeted with sagebrush, cacti, yucca, and buffalo grass. In the distance he saw spots of brown that began to move, and he snatched a pair of binoculars he had traded for at Bent's Fort and lifted them to scan the distant flats. He grinned as the brown spots showed themselves to be a small herd of buffalo, grazing on the grasses and meandering slowly northward.

He easily fell into the practice of wandering men and spoke to his horse, "Well, Dusty, if they weren't so far away I might try for one, but they're purt'near big as you an' I ain't sure what we'd do with all that meat. Mule's loaded with all our gear an' supplies, an' I ain't givin' up muh saddle for nuthin', so, reckon we best let 'em be." He chuckled and reached down to stroke the neck of the big Percheron gelding. He turned to look to his left where the trail ducked into the cottonwoods and reined Dusty that direction. "That there must be where we're to cross that river, Dusty. That ol' trapper fella we was talkin' to in the fort back yonder said we'd cross over, then bear to the southwest. Those two snow-capped mountains to the south there are what he called the Spanish Peaks, and that smaller one north of 'em don't have a name right yet, but he said it's the one with the white top. We're to split the distance an' foller the Cucharas River, then the next crick that comes from the north he called the Sangre de Cristo, same as that long stretch of high mountains. He said that'll get us into the San Luis Valley and from there, well, we'll just go wherever we want to!" He chuckled to himself feeling a freedom never before known.

His youth had been spent in company housing while his father and brother worked in the coal mines, and he eventually followed them. They had never known the freedom of having their own home, or even buying anything from anywhere but the company store with scrip. But he and his father had both worked odd jobs, made side money, and saved it all. Now he alone would enjoy the freedom bought at such a price.

The river was no deeper than the knees of the big horse and mule and they quickly crossed and pushed on toward the mountains. The old-timer at the fort said it would be most of three days just getting to the mountains, another day crossing over and into the valley. Red was in no hurry, he wanted to enjoy every moment and memory of his journey. He let Dusty have his head as they followed the two-track wagon trail toward the mountains. He looked around at the scattered, blue-tinted sage, the gnarly greasewood, and the patches of prickly pear cactus. The random patches of bunchgrass, grama, and buffalo grass showed faint remnants of green as spring had faded and summer was crowding the land. Dusty sidestepped when a long-eared jackrabbit jumped from the sage with a scrawny coyote in hot pursuit, but Red, having instinctively grabbed the saddle horn, kept his seat and laughed at the disappearing coyote. But he grew watchful, the old-timer had told him to keep his eyes open, "Cuz every'thin' out'chere will either bite'cha, kick'ya, gore'ya, sting'ya, scalp'ya, an' all'em will try to kill ya!"

Dusty stopped suddenly, his ears pricked and his head dropping as he started backstepping and Red saw the biggest diamondback rattlesnake slithering across the trail. The flickering tongue always moving as he wound his way across the trail, his nose touching the edge of the sage on the left and his tail just leaving the grass on the right. Dusty nervously trembled and Red reached down to stroke his neck, "Good boy Dusty. That thing's big 'nuff to kill us both," and continued to stroke his neck as he settled down.

They pushed on, stopping only when they crossed a draw that offered a break from the hot sun, or water for a drink. He was sparing with the water in the water bags, a lesson he learned while with the freighters as they crossed the flats before Bent's Fort. As the sun dropped behind the distant mountains, Red came to a bit of a creek that showed evidence of spring floodwaters but now carried a trickle of water that was only a few inches deep and not more than a couple feet wide, but it was enough, and the scraggly cottonwoods offered some protection for the night's camp.

He enjoyed making his first camp on the trail. Although it was not always his choice, he had come to be a solitary man. All too often when he sought the company of others, his size became the focus of attention and lesser men would often want to prove themselves against the big man by picking a fight or making crude remarks, assuming that anyone so big was also stupid, but Red was a quiet and studious man who enjoyed reading and always sought to learn and his knowledge and wisdom became another obstacle to others that might otherwise seek his company. He remembered the first and last time he entered a saloon he was looking for his Pa and the town bully tried to pick a fight. When the man took a swing at Red, who was a head taller than the saloon tough guy, Red caught his fist in his big palm, gripped it and squeezed as he bent the man's fist back, driving the wincing and whining tough to the ground. Red released him, turned away and the man tried to bust a chair over his back, but Red shrugged it off, turned and grabbed the tough by his shirt and belt, lifted him overhead and dropped him on the bar. With a growl, Red slid the man down the bar, to send him sailing through the window to land in a heap on the boardwalk. Red shook his head at the memory, glad that was far in his past.

While traveling with the freighters from Westport on the Santa Fe Trail, he watched and learned and now applied much of what he learned. He whipped up some cornmeal biscuits, lay them in the Dutch oven and set the cast-iron oven to the side of the cookfire, shoveled some coals to the side, set the pot atop, put more coals on the lid, and set about fixing a pot of coffee, a pot of stew made from pork belly, potatoes, and beans bought at Bent's Fort. He sat back, glanced to the horse and mule grazing at the edge of the creek on the strip of greenery beside the creek, and enjoyed the sights and sounds of the plains.

As the water in the coffeepot started steaming, he reached for the pot, pulled it back and dropped a small handful of coffee into the water, replaced the lid and slid the pot back on the rock for the flames to continue licking at the base and start the perking. As he sat back, he sensed, more than saw, something near the cottonwood saplings, and loosened his jacket to give access to his Colt Dragoon pistol. He casually turned to look toward the trees and saw the skinny, half-naked form of a boy with long black hair hanging in braids and touching his shoulders, a breechcloth and buckskin leggings, and with his arms folded across his chest. The youngster glared at Red and muttered something in a language that Red did not understand.

Red nodded to the youngster, motioned for him to come closer, and asked, making crude sign and motions, "Are you hungry? Need something to eat?"

The youngster frowned, looked at Red and at the hanging pot that was boiling with the stew, and motioned to his mouth and said, "*tügüynaru'ayü.*"

Red nodded, "Soon, we eat." He motioned for the boy to sit, and the young man crossed his arms over his chest and stood with head held high, feet apart, and a proud look on his face. Red leaned forward to check the stew, stirred it and replaced the lid. Looked at the coffeepot beginning its dance and glanced to the Dutch oven, then sat back to wait.

He touched his chest, said, "I am Red," then pointed to the youngster, "Who are you?"

"*Yogovüch*—coyote." Red was surprised but pleased to hear him say the English word, Coyote.

"Do you speak English?" he asked.

The young man nodded, "Some, why are you called Red?"

Red pointed to his beard and hair, grinning. "Are you alone?" asked Red, frowning, thinking the boy was young to be all alone in the empty land, wondering about his people.

"My mother there," he pointed up the creek bed.

"Is she alright? Does she need help?"

Company

RED LOOKED AT THE YOUNGSTER, FROWNED, "GO GET YOUR mother, bring her, and we will eat together," suggested Red, wondering about the absent woman.

The stoic youngster looked at Red, unmoving, and with a glance to the hanging pot, he looked at Red, turned to point to the trees, "She is there."

Red looked to the edge of the firelight and saw a hint of movement by the cottonwood saplings and motioned for the woman to come near. Nothing stirred, no sound came for a couple moments, then movement showed, and a woman stepped into the firelight. She was younger than Red expected, although he did not know exactly what he expected, but she did appear too young to have a child the age of the boy. With long black hair that shone in the firelight, her face showed welts and her left eye was swollen almost shut. Her lip was swollen, and a dark bruise showed on her right cheek. Blood showed on the buckskin tunic and her fringed leggings showed mud on the knees. She stood with hands at her sides and looked from Coyote to Red and dropped her eyes.

Red motioned for her to come forward, "Come, we will

eat. Then we might need to see what we can do about your injuries." He turned to Coyote, "Does she understand?"

Coyote nodded, "Some."

Red frowned, "What happened?"

"Comancheros. They attacked the wagon train, ran away and came to the camp of my father and others. They attacked, stole everything, killed my father and others."

"Comancheros—they are the Mexicans that trade with the Comanches?"

"Yes. But we are not Comanche—we are Ute! Mouache Ute."

Red turned to the woman, "I am called Red, what is your name?"

"I am Yellow Bird."

"Did the Comancheros do this to you?"

"Yes, when they killed my man."

"Sit, let's eat first, then we'll see to your injuries."

When Red thought the stew and coffee were done, he stood and went to the pot. Until then, he had remained seated and when he stood tall, both the boy and the woman leaned back and looked wide-eyed at this big man who was bigger than anyone they had ever seen and his massive size with the broad shoulders and deep chest with whiskers that bounced when he laughed kept the two spellbound. He paid little attention to their wonder and filled the lid of the pot and a plate with food, giving the lid to the young man and the plate to the woman. He poured himself a cup of coffee and sat down to watch the two very hungry natives feed themselves.

He pulled the Dutch oven away from the fire, lifted the lid with his gloved hand and dumped the coals aside, then reached in and pulled out some of the biscuits, gave one to each of his guests, and took two for himself, replaced the lid and sat down to enjoy his biscuits. As they ate, they talked and Red learned that their camp had only three families, and all were killed, and Yellow Bird was left for dead while

Coyote had been away hunting for rabbits for supper and returned to find the camp destroyed and bodies strewn about.

Red looked at the woman, "You will stay with me until we can get you back to your people. They say there is a settlement near the mountains, maybe we can get you a horse or two there, but until then, you can ride with me, and the boy can ride the mule."

"Why would you do this?" asked Yellow Bird.

"It's the right thing to do and if it were me, I would hope you would help me."

Yellow Bird frowned at the big man, stood, and began cleaning the pots and more. Red watched her, thinking that before the beating she was a beautiful woman, but women never paid attention to him, and he turned his thoughts to the trail and the settlement he had been told about by the old-timer at the fort.

La Plaza de los Leones was little more than a trading post recently built with an adjoining cabin for the trader, Don Miguel Antonio de Leon. Two other log buildings sat nearby and a larger barn with an attached corral made up the town's livery. When Red rode into the little settlement with a native woman behind him, the few settlers who all appeared to be Mexican, stared. He paid them no mind and reined up at the livery, saw a man working at an anvil and called out, "Mornin'! Got'ny horses for sale?" he asked.

The liveryman stopped his work, looked up at Red, and asked, "Got'ny money?"

"Some. Need a horse or two for the woman here."

"You want a horse for that Indian?" asked the man, somewhat incredulous that this white man would be traveling with a native woman.

"That's right. Some Comancheros hit their camp and killed all of 'em but her and the boy."

"I got some horses, but I ain't gonna sell 'em to you if that's what they're for," growled the liveryman.

Red shook his head, stepped down and walked closer to the man who held a big hammer that he was using on the horseshoe on the anvil. Red stepped close and spoke softly, "Now, your skin and her skin is about the same color, she has the same color hair that you do, and she needs a horse." He glanced through the barn to see a corral with four horses standing at the rail, "How much for that buckskin?"

"I told you..." started the man, until Red leaned forward, putting his weight on the handle of the hammer in the man's hand. The liveryman looked at Red, down at his meaty paw on the hammer and began to feel his fingers smashing between the hammer and the anvil. He gasped a short breath, winced, and said, "Ten dollars!"

Red grinned, stepped back and reached into the pocket of his whipcord britches and pulled out a ten-dollar gold piece and handed it to the man, "That includes a blanket and bosal, right?"

The man nodded, pocketed the coin, and rubbed his fingers before returning to his work.

Red grabbed a bosal from a nail, a blanket from the rail, and went to the corral to catch up the buckskin mare. He led the horse through the barn, stopped beside the grey Percheron and lifted Yellow Bird from his horse to hers, smiled and nodded, swung back aboard Dusty, and led the way from the little settlement.

"The valley is called San Luis Valley by the people of San Luis and the mountains are called the Sangre de Cristo Mountains. Those are names given to them by the people that settled in San Luis, this is what we were told by the black robes. My people tell of the black robes and their people that used the Capote Ute people as slaves to dig in the mountains for their yellow metal. My people tell of the time when they turned on the black robes and those that wore metal on their chests and heads and when they killed the black robe, he looked at the mountains and pointed because the mountains were made red by the sun and called them Sangre de Cristo."

"Is that how you learned to speak English?" asked Red.

"My mother learned from them and taught me, and I taught my son," answered Yellow Bird, nodding to Coyote.

"And where are your people now?"

"They are at the summer camp in the north of the mountains west of the valley."

"How long before we get there?"

She held out her hand, all fingers extended, "This many days."

They had stopped at the base of the long white-topped ridge. The trail lay in the bottom of a long valley that sided the long ridge, following the little creek that fell from the higher mountains. The air was cool, and the aspen trees were showing the pale green of their new leaves as the breeze whispered down the valley, ruffling all the leaves and giving the trees the nickname of quakies. They reminded Red of the white-barked birch he knew in the East, but these were smaller and grew in thicker clusters, adding contrast to the black timber of the pines that cloaked the magnificent mountains. They had moved off the trail and deeper into the trees that rode the banks of the little creek. A clearing offered grass and the trees afforded cover. Red had been feeling the rising of his hackles which told him someone was watching or following them, and he wanted no surprises.

Yellow Bird offered to take on the duties of cooking their meal and Red willingly obliged. He took his binoculars and Sharps with him as he climbed the shoulder of the ridge behind them that lay parallel to the white-capped bigger ridge that had been their landmark throughout the day. He was anxious to get a better look at their backtrail. He was not certain they were followed, and he could not imagine who it could be, but he had learned long ago to take nothing for granted. He made his way stealthily through the trees, a habit he learned as a boy when he wanted to be away from others, until he came to a slight escarpment with scraggly piñon trees that clung tenaciously to the rocks. With the bigger of the trees for cover, he went to one knee and began to search the long valley for sign of followers. "There!" he whispered to himself. He watched as four riders came into view, the leader leaning low to search the ground for tracks.

"There! Ain't hard to follow the tracks of that big horse!" declared the leader. He wore a wide sombrero, the short bolero jacket common to vaqueros, and rode a saddle with the big flat horn common to the Mexican style. The others were attired in a similar manner and Red guessed them to be the Comancheros that had attacked the wagon train and the camp of the Ute.

One of the men asked, "Will we wait until they are asleep?"

"No! I want that woman!" declared the leader, snarling as he spoke.

"But that man is a giant!" declared one of the men.

"No man is bigger than this!" declared the leader, lifting his pistol before him as he dug spurs into the ribs of his horse that lunged forward, leading the way.

Red shook his head, and although he had not heard the words of the men, he knew what they were doing. These were the Comancheros who were used to taking whatever they wanted and leaving nothing but ashes and dead bodies behind. He came to his feet and quickly returned to the camp. He told Yellow Bird about the men and what he would do and what she should do when they came. She nodded, "They will try to kill you! These are evil men!"

Surprise

"Manuel—they left the trail here!" declared the second man, Alonzo. He was on one knee, looking at the tracks of the big horse and the pack mule. He looked in the direction taken by the tracks, slowly stood as he looked, "There's nothing up there—they must have made camp."

The leader, Manuel, stood in his stirrups to look up the narrow valley and saw where the aspen lay in a narrow ravine and the darker timber covered the hillside. He sat in the saddle, looked to the other men, "There! I see smoke. They are making their supper," he cackled, laughing, "they are making *our* supper! Come." He nudged his mount to the faint trail toward the smoke, believing they were approaching unseen and unheard. As they neared the camp, Manuel called out, "Hello the camp!"

"What you want?" answered the voice of the woman.

Manuel grinned as he glanced to his men, "We are hungry and could smell your cooking. We would like to share your meal!"

The camp was still obscured in the trees and the four men slowly nudged their horses forward, Manuel and Alonzo in the front, with pistols drawn but held low behind the pommel of their saddles. Federico and Juan followed close behind, Juan with his new Henry repeater that lay across his pommel and Federico with his hand on the butt of his Remington revolver. They pushed through the trees and Manuel stopped at the edge of the clearing, leaving the others still in the trees. Manuel grinned, looking around, asked, "Where is your man —the beeg one?"

A deep voice rumbled from behind, "Here! With my Sharps sighted on the back of your head, señor!" Manuel started to turn as did the others, each gripping their weapons, but Red warned, "No! Don't move! The first one that turns— dies!" he declared. Red was behind the big trunk of a towering ponderosa, down on one knee, with just the barrel of the Sharps showing at the side of the red-barked tree.

"But señor, you only have one bullet in that Sharps and there are four of us! If you shoot one, the others will shoot you and your woman and the boy! You don' wan' them to die, do you?"

"She's not my woman, and he's not my boy. But if anyone moves, you will be the first to die and you won't know what happens to the woman and the boy!"

Manuel tried to tell his men what to do, but his whisper was heard by Red, and as Manuel started to lift his pistol the Sharps bucked and roared, the blast echoing across the narrow draw and the bullet tore off the top of Manuel's head. The bark of the rifle startled the horses and the other three men, although trying to turn around to face the threat behind them, fought to control the animals.

Red let loose a shrill whistle and the big Percheron responded immediately and charged through the melee of men fighting with their horses, knocking them to the side as he barreled between them. Red stepped to the side of Federico and knocked him from his saddle with a blow from the butt of the Sharps, dropping Federico in a clump between the high-stepping horses. Red shoved against the horse, knocking it into the side of Juan's mount, trampling on Federico and jostling Juan sideways in the saddle, but as Juan turned he stared down the barrel of Red's Colt Dragoon, the one-eyed monster stared death at Juan, and he dropped his rifle and lifted his hands high, "No, señor! No!" he declared. Red motioned for him to step down just as Alonzo turned toward Red, but Red swung the Colt his direction to warn the man, but the glare in Alonzo's eyes showed red and Red dropped the hammer on the Colt, the pistol bucked and roared and the bullet shattered the sternum of Alonzo, taking a fist-sized chunk of flesh with it as it blasted out his back. Alonzo slid to the ground, sightless eyes staring at the dirt.

Red looked at Juan, "If you want to live, take your partner," motioning to the battered Federico that struggled to come to his feet, "and leave this country. If I see you again, you're dead!"

"Si, señor, gracias señor," replied Juan, offering a hand to Federico and helping him to mount his horse. With the muzzle of the Dragoon in Red's hands staring at them, the two men turned back into the trees and dug spurs into the ribs of their mounts, the clatter of the horses' hooves racketing down the long valley to fade away in the distance.

Red dragged the bodies of the two men away, throwing them into a dry gulch that came from the high ridge, caved the bank over their bodies, and returned to the camp. Coyote had caught up the horses and now four horses and one mule stood watching as Red came back into the camp. He grinned, looked at Yellow Bird, "Supper ready?"

The meal began in silence, with Yellow Bird often glancing to Red, a frown clouding her face until she asked, "What did you do with them?" nodding toward the trees where he went with the bodies.

"They're buried down yonder in a dry gulch."

"What happens to them now?" she asked.

Red frowned and looked at Yellow Bird, "What do you mean? They're dead and buried, nothing can happen."

"My people believe that their spirit is still around for a few days, then they go to another place. If Senawahv, the great creator, allows, they will live on as a spirit. That is why our people mourn and place their things at their burial place. Is that what you believe?"

Red dropped his eyes and thought a moment, "No, what I believe is what my mother taught me as a youngster and what I read in God's word, the Bible. He, the great creator, has given us this," he paused and dug into his saddlebags to withdraw a well-worn Bible, held it up for her to see, "so we would know what is right and wrong. He tells us in this book what we must do and be to get to Heaven, the special and wonderful place He has prepared for us for after we die." He paused and began flipping through the pages, "And He also tells us that men like that, men that do not know nor believe in God and His son, Jesus, have a place where they go, and it's a terrible place of punishment."

Yellow Bird sat aside the trencher she had carved out of a wide piece of wood and now used as a plate, looked at Red, and asked, "Do they ever leave that place?"

Red slowly shook his head, "No, it is forever. It's dark, it's hot, and there is no relief from the pain and agony."

"What does He say we must do so we will not go there?" she asked. Her interest had prompted Coyote to come nearer and pay close attention.

"Well, my Momma taught me about that, and I'll try to remember the right verses here in the Good Book. She said we need to admit we're sinners, that's when we have done some bad things, you know, telling lies, not doin' what we should and such. That ever true about you, you know, done some things that were wrong?"

Yellow Bird dropped her eyes and nodded her head.

Red continued, "Then we need to know that because

we've done wrong, what we deserve is to go to Hell forever, that's the place where the evil ones go. But..." He grinned and looked to Yellow Bird and Coyote. "God, the Creator, loves us, and does not want us to go there. So, He made a way so we would not have to, and that way is what His Son Jesus did for us. You see, because we're sinners, we deserve Hell, but because He loves us, He sent his son to pay the price for our sin so we would not have to, He, Jesus, went to the cross and shed his blood to pay that price." He paused, began flipping some pages in the Bible and stopped, ran his finger down the page and said, "Now it says right here in Romans chapter six, *The wages of sin is death*...now that means because we're sinners and have done those bad things, then the penalty is death, and that means more than just dying, it's after we die that we spend eternity or the rest of time in that place called Hell. But it goes on, *but the gift of God is eternal life through Jesus Christ our Lord*. See, it is a gift paid for by Jesus's blood on the cross and that gift is to live forever in Heaven with Jesus."

"But if it is a gift, how do we get such a gift?" asked Yellow Bird, inching closer to Red, her elbows on her knees as she looked at him.

"That's the best part and He tells us a few chapters later in chapter ten that all we have to do is believe in our heart and ask him in prayer for that gift."

"I don't understand."

"Do you believe what I've told you about Jesus and that the gift of eternal life is offered to you?"

"Yes, yes, I believe what you say."

"Then, just like any gift, it does nothing until we accept it."

"My people believe that if you accept a gift, you must return with a gift as good or better. How can we do that with the Creator?"

Red paused, thinking about it, and a slow smile began to

spread across his face, "That is what else He teaches us. That if we believe with our hearts and accept the gift of eternal life, then the way we show our love for Him is to live our lives in a good way and tell others about His gift so they, too, can go to Heaven."

"Will you tell me how to accept that gift?" asked Yellow Bird, and Coyote nodded enthusiastically and added, "Me too!"

"Yes, we pray. Now I will pray, and if you believe with your heart, then just repeat this prayer after me. Dear God…" and he continued in prayer, letting them echo his words, as he asked forgiveness for sins, and that he believed in his heart that Jesus paid the price for him, and that he wanted that gift of eternal life so he would have a home in Heaven forever. When he finished, he said "Amen" and Yellow Bird and Coyote echoed those words. When they opened their eyes and looked at Red with a smile, he too was showing a broad smile and they hugged one another, happy with their decision.

Red started to put the Bible away when Yellow Bird asked, "Could you teach us to read those tracks?"

Red frowned until Yellow Bird pointed to the Bible. He grinned, "You mean these words?" He opened the Bible and pointed to the print on the paper.

"Yes, those are like tracks that we follow to go to different places. We would like to know those things."

"I'll do my best, but it takes a long time to learn to read."

She smiled and nodded and began putting the pans and such away for the night.

Home

I<small>T WAS LATE ON THE THIRD DAY AFTER THE ENCOUNTER WITH THE</small> Comancheros that Yellow Bird pointed to the hills that rose on the west edge of the San Luis Valley, "There is the land of my people. Our village is in those hills, but it would not be good for you to come."

It had been an extraordinary three days for the man from the Pennsylvania coal mines. They rounded the flank of Mount Blanca, the snowcapped peak that stood tall and proud as its white pinnacles scratched the blue of the cloudless sky, and Yellow Bird pointed out Fort Garland, the military fort that was built to protect the white settlers that came into and through the San Luis Valley. They turned north and rode the tree-line skirts of the Sangre de Cristo Mountain range that stretched into the north like a parade of stiff-backed soldiers marching into the unknown. With the wide grassy valley below the Sangres and the foothills of the San Juan Mountains to the west, this was the most beautiful land in the eyes of the wandering and wondering Red Pierce he had ever seen.

With every step of his big Percheron, he reveled in the wild beauty of the land and more than anything else, he appreciated the absence of people. For those three days the only living things they saw were an abundance of mule deer, a herd of pronghorn antelope that ran through the sage and grasses, a bunch of elk that came down from the higher mountains to graze on the grasses of the valley, and one glimpse of some full-curl rams of a small herd of mountain sheep. And the valley showed an abundance of long-eared jackrabbits, cottontails, coyote, bobcats, and the nighttime howl of wolves to lull them to sleep. It was a marvelous land and Red basked in it all.

After they passed the wonder of natural hot springs where Yellow Bird said her people often came, they rode up a wide break in the foothills, following a creek that would one day be known as Kerber Creek. As it cut through the foothills, a wide basin beckoned and Red reined up, looking about. He asked Yellow Bird, "How far is your village?"

"It is beyond that mountain, a basin with water and more is where we make our summer camp."

"So, less than a day?"

"Yes."

"So, if I decide to stay here, build me a cabin back in those trees, and make this my home, will you come visit me?" he asked, letting a slow grin part his whiskers.

Yellow Bird dropped her eyes and said, "My time of mourning for my man is not over." She lifted her eyes, "But I would like to come visit you after," and smiled.

Red nodded, smiling, "And how long will that be?"

"Before the snow comes."

"I have much to learn, and you could show me many things. It would be good for us to be together."

"Perhaps. But I must go now."

———

I⊤ was an ancient trail used by the ancestors of the Mouache people. It followed the contours of the land, always above the creek bottom and the many beaver dams that housed the flat-tailed rodents. The trail usually kept inside the tree line, but low enough to afford a view of the valley bottom. Red spotted a sizable grove of aspen that painted the western slope of a long high-rising ridge and after looking it over, found just the right shoulder that was back in the black timber opposite the aspen, and decided this would be his home.

It was near the headwaters of the creek, but still within the runoff and high enough on the hill to avoid any spring floods. There fir, spruce and pine were in abundance but Red chose to cut randomly, choosing his logs for their length, straight-ness, and size, but never taking too many in any one stand, avoiding giving away his presence. He labored long and hard, snaking the felled trees back to his homesite, cutting and trimming them to fit, as he hoisted the first five rows of logs for the rectangular cabin. He used his ingenuity and fashioned a hoist to lift one end then the other of the bigger logs that stacked higher than most cabins. He wanted enough headroom inside for his tall frame, and even the doors and window openings were taller than the norm.

With a good stand of lodgepole pine, he cut the long straight poles for the rafters and beams, and soon had his house built. He would spend the cold winter months inside making the furniture and cabinets to finish things off, but for now, he fashioned a crude bed, chair, and table that would serve his purposes for the present. Now he wanted to spend his time outside. He would do a little prospecting, hunting for his winter stores, and learning the lay of the land of his new home.

The stream that chuckled below the cabin was backed up in several places with beaver ponds and Red slowly walked along the grassy bank that lay between the stream and the thickets of aspen. It was a bright and beautiful day, the lazy breeze whispered through the quakies, ruffling the leaves providing harmony to the chattering chipmunks and chirping redwing blackbirds. He bent to pick up a flat rock to skip across the calm water of the bigger beaver pond but stopped when he saw movement on the far bank. From the shadows ambled a brown mountain of fur, head swinging side to side, a low rumble coming from deep in the broad chest. Behind the big sow grizzly, scampered a furry cub who would stop and swat at anything and everything, roll in the grass and chase after his mom.

Red paused, watching the denizens of the mountains scamper about and stepped closer to water's edge, enjoying the symphony of sounds—the chuckle of the stream, the whisper of the wind, the chatter of chipmunks, the caw of the blackbirds—but suddenly all fell silent. A leaf-rattling roar came from the edge of the black timber as a giant of a bear stood on hind legs, pawed at the air with his dinner-plate-sized paws as he snapped his jaws and let another roar sweep across the grassy bank. The sow grizzly turned to find her cub, barked at it to come close, and stood between the cub and the big boar.

With another challenging roar, the massive boar dropped to all fours and charged the sow. Red had learned from the freighters that grizzlies would often kill the cubs to cause the sow to come back into season for breeding, but this sow was determined to protect her offspring. As the boar lumbered near, snapping his jaws and growling, the sow sidestepped, often reaching out to slap at the boar, but the big beast would not be thwarted and charged the sow, bowling her over and grabbing a mouth full of fur at her neck. He tried to mount the sow, but she dropped her haunches, spun around and took a mouthful of fur and hide, burying her teeth in the back of the boar's neck, refusing to let go, but the boar rolled, bringing her with him and forcing her to loose her grip. When he came to his feet, he charged the cub, but the blast of the

Sharps rifle in the hands of Red sent a .52-caliber slug into the front shoulder of the beast, causing him to stumble, but quickly come to his feet, rise to his full height on his hind legs and bite at his wound as if it were some troublesome bug bite.

The sow took the offense and charged into the big boar, knocking him to his back, as both fought to sink their teeth into the throats of the other. They growled, snapped, barked, bit, clawed and used their weight to drive the other to the ground. They churned up the grass with their battle, making the flat of the small meadow look more like the plowed field of a farmer. Red wanted to finish it but could not get another clear shot with his Sharps. He saw the cub scamper away, turn and rise on his hind legs, and at a bark from his mother, scamper up the trunk of the lone ponderosa to watch the fight from on high.

The fight seemed to last for hours, but a quick glance to the sun told Red it had been less than a half hour when the battle waned. The big boar straddled the downed sow, now on her back, with his teeth sunk in her throat. He growled and grumbled, shook his head side to side, but the life had slipped from the sow and the boar knew she was dead. He released his bite, lifted his head, cocked it to the side to look at the sow, nudged her jaw with his nose, then slowly stepped back. He rose to his hind legs, looking around for the cub, but the little furball was high in the ponderosa, staying still and quiet. The boar caught the scent of the cub and ambled over to the tree, rose up on his hind legs and stretched as high as he could and began to claw the red bark to mark his territory as if warning the cub of his impending fate.

Red thought about shooting the boar but let him go and watched as the beast ambled into the black timber. Red looked to the big tree, saw no movement, and started to cross the chuckling stream and go closer, but as he took his first step into the water, his eye caught a sparkle of color reflecting the sunlight from the shallows below a big rock. He paused, leaned down to look closer, reached into the water and brought up a handful of sandy silt that sparkled in the sun as he looked at the flakes of gold. A slow grin began to paint his face and he glanced to the tree, saw no movement, looked back at the gold, and said, "Looks like I've got some work to do!"

He returned to the cabin, fetched his shovel, gold pans, a leather pouch, and returned to the creek. He began to pan the silt, slowly washing the sand and silt out with the swirling motion and when there were only a few flakes of gold left, he carefully picked them out and put them in the pouch and did it all again. After a couple hours of panning, he sat back on the edge of the creek bank, looking around and glanced to the ponderosa to see the cub slowly working his way down. But movement at the corner of his eye caught his attention and Red turned to look at the bald ridge above and further downstream to see a lone warrior about a quarter mile distant, sitting astride his mount, and looking directly at him. Red did not move, but watched the man until he reined his mount away and disappeared over the ridge. A quick glance reassured Red his Sharps was within arm's reach and his pistol still hung in the holster on his hip.

In the few hours of panning, he had accumulated about a shallow palm full of gold flakes, one nugget about the size of the fingernail on his little finger, and he hung the pouch from his belt. Reached for the pan and looked up to see the cub ambling toward the body of his mother. Red watched as the foundling nudged the body, whimpered, and tried to nurse. Red shook his head, feeling the fear and lonesomeness of the cub, wondering what he could do, but he failed to come up with an answer and continued panning.

Red sat back on the bank and was surprised to look across the water to see the cub sitting on his haunches, cocking his head to the side, and watching as Red picked the flakes from the pan and added them to the pouch. "Whaddya say, boy?

What'chu gonna do now? Got'ny other family to go to, maybe a den or sumpin'?"

The cub cocked his head side to side as he listened to the deep bass voice of the big man that was almost as big as his mother and had fur almost the same color. The growling voice was friendly and comforting, and the confused cub crawled a little closer, bellied down and with his chin on his front paws, watched Red as he panned the gold.

Family

RED SAT ON HIS PORCH—THE LOG BENCH STRETCHED UNDER THE shuttered window beside the door. He frowned as he watched two riders coming up the trail and turn toward the trees that sheltered his cabin, he had watched when they crossed the far ridge and dropped into the bottom to take the trail. He reached to his right to touch the stock of the Sharps, but before picking it up, he thought he recognized the riders, and a slow grin painted his face. Across the creek-bottomed draw that lay below his cabin, the quakies were fluttering their gold leaves, the cool breeze foretelling the coming of winter, and the cloudy sky hinted at the first snowstorm for the valley. He stood, one hand on the porch post, the other on his hip, as he called out, "Welcome, Yellow Bird, Coyote. I was wondering when you would come visit."

As they reined up before the cabin, Red added, "Step down, come take a look at my home!" But Yellow Bird frowned, glanced from Coyote to Red as she pointed to the porch, wide-eyed. Red chuckled, "Aw, that's Tugs, I adopted him a couple months ago. He won't hurt'chu!"

But Yellow Bird hesitated, watching the grizzly cub that was hip high on Red and stood beside him, leaning against his leg. Red dropped a hand to the cub's head and watched as Yellow Bird and Coyote slowly climbed down and started toward the cabin. Red moved aside, keeping Tugs behind him and motioned for his visitors to go inside and followed after them, the cub at his heels.

Once inside, he pointed out the loft as a sleeping area, the back room which was a bedroom, "And the rest of this will be where we cook the meals, eat, and such. The fireplace there will keep the whole place warm." He chuckled as he glanced to Tugs, "It took him a while to get used to the fire, but he sleeps near the door as far away as he can."

Red looked at Yellow Bird who was smiling and looking around. He remembered what she looked like when he first found her and now she was healed up and looking prettier than ever. Her long black hair hung loosely over her shoulders, a sheen that added to her beauty and her eyes were bright and showed a hint of mischief as her petite mouth tugged at the corners as she looked at him. Red asked, "Will you stay a while? I can start teaching you to read, like you asked."

"Do you mean the tracks in the book?"

"That's right. There's plenty of room. You can have that room," nodding to the door of the bedroom, "I'll sleep out here with Tugs and Coyote can take the loft," nodding toward the ladder that led to the loft.

"We will stay a while," agreed Yellow Bird, a broad smile splitting her face as she looked up at Red.

"Good, good. Then let's put your horses in the corral and your gear in the lean-to. Dusty and Mule will probably like the company."

At the end of the third day, Red and Yellow Bird sat together on the porch, enjoying the evening air and the colors of the mountains. Red looked at her, "Yellow Bird, what do your people do when they want to be married, you know, to become man and wife and start a family?"

Yellow Bird frowned, looked at Red, "They go into the same lodge and are one. What do your people do?"

"It's a little more than that. They have to have a minister, a black robe as you call them, say some words over them and they agree to be husband and wife and move in together."

"Is that what you want to do?" asked Yellow Bird, smiling coyly at the big man.

Red dropped his eyes, felt the warmth climbing his neck and chuckled, "Thought about it," he admitted. "I would like to have you for my wife, but there's no minister around hereabouts."

"That is why we came. The brother of my man wanted me to be his second woman, but I do not want that. When you helped us return to my people, I was grateful, but after we parted, I wanted to return to you. I believe you are a good man and I want you for my man." She smiled, dropped her eyes, and waited for Red to respond.

Red sat very still, looking at her and marveling at how beautiful she was and how surprised he was that she wanted to be with him. He had never known a woman, nor spent any time with any woman, but with Yellow Bird, she seemed to be a part of him, a part he did not want to lose. "Do you need to return to your people to tell them, or to get any of your things?"

"No, I think those that are close to me know my thoughts about you."

"Then I guess I better get busy making the bed for our bedroom," declared a grinning Red as he rose from the bench, but Yellow Bird stopped him and pointed to the trail in the far draw. Three riders were approaching, apparently following the tracks left by Yellow Bird and Coyote. Red picked up his Sharps, checked the load, drew his pistol from the holster and checked the loads and caps, replaced the pistol and stood at the edge of the porch above the steps and waited for the three men to come. As they neared, Yellow Bird stood behind Red and said, "That is Black Hawk, the brother of him who was my man."

Red slowly nodded, held his rifle across his chest and cradled in the crook of his left arm, his right hand on the grip. The one called Black Hawk was in the lead and was an impressive figure. With his hairpipe bone breastplate dangling over his broad chest, a silver band on his upper left arm, a war shield on his left hand and a war lance in his right that had feathers and scalp locks dangling, the scowl on his face showed a vehement hatred as his nostrils flared and he growled, "That is my woman! Yellow Bird! Come with me, now!"

Red stepped forward, eased down the three steps of the porch, and walked closer to the three men, although still on higher ground. He looked at Black Hawk, "She is my woman! She has made her choice. Now we can be friends, or we can be enemies. You can get down right now and we can settle this, or..." and shrugged, grinning.

Black Hawk glared at Red, lifted his lance and tossed it in the air to catch it in a throwing position, but before he could catch the lance, Red jerked him off his horse, dropped his rifle, and turned Black Hawk with his back to Red's chest and wrapped his arms around him, pinning Black Hawk's arms to his side. It happened so fast, Black Hawk's eyes flared, and fear showed, but he struggled to free himself, but Red just chuckled, "You ain't goin' nowhere. But I got a friend and it's comin' on to his feedin' time. Maybe I'll just feed you to Tugs."

Black Hawk kicked out with his feet, using all his weight in an effort to drop beneath Red's arms, but Red's grip was too tight, and he carried the kicking captive toward the porch and called out, "Tugs! Hey Tugs! Suppertime!"

The big grizzly cub, now a yearling and as big as a typical black bear, ambled around the corner of the cabin and rose to his full height on his hind legs, his front paws swiping at the air before him as he growled and snapped his jaws. The two warriors that still sat their mounts shouted, "Aiiieeeee! The bear!" pointing to Tugs and trying to bring their horses under control. It is the natural response of any prey to take flight and the struggle of the warriors was to no avail and their horses reared up, turned away and fled through the trees, followed by the riderless mount of Black Hawk.

Red spoke low into the ear of Black Hawk, "So, you wanna feed the bear or be friends?"

Black Hawk growled, still struggling to free himself from the grip of Red, then stopped his struggle as he looked at the grizzly, then twisted his head to try to look at Red, saw a grinning Yellow Bird on the porch, "What is this man that talks to the bears?"

"He is my man, and we will stay with him. If you agree to be friends, he will let you go and return to our people and warn them of this great man and his powers!"

"I will go!" answered Black Hawk, scowling at the woman. Red chuckled, released and said, "Your shield and lance are there. If you hurry, you might catch up to your friends."

They watched as the proud but humbled warrior trotted through the trees, chasing after his horse and fellow warriors.

———

IT WAS after the first snow that another visitor came to the cabin. She was the sister of Yellow Bird and was giddy with happiness to find her sister so happy. She told her that the word had spread about her man and the people were calling him Big Bear. Yellow Bird smiled, "And Coyote has made his first kill, and we have given him the name Little Bear," she giggled, put her hand on her belly and smiled, "And we will have another cub in our den after greenup."

Red stepped behind her, wrapped his big arms around the

tiny woman and with a broad smile added, "And Tugs will be big enough to go looking for his own mate and den about that time too!"

They were a happy family, more than Red ever imagined, but now he could not imagine a life without them.

Who the Hell? What the Hell?

L. J. Martin

1

I STAND IN AWE, STARING AT THE RECENTLY SHAVED AND groomed man, seeing myself staring back, a man seemingly equally astounded. But I must begin at the beginning.

The Transcontinental Railroad, what an accomplishment! I'd only arrived in Sacramento three days ago, then by side-wheeler down the Sacramento River to San Francisco just yesterday. Never in my thirty-four years did I think anything would exceed the marvel of the wedding of east to west that is those long set of rails across prairies and along the vertical granite shoulders of the towering Sierra Mountains...until this morning. At least in what rotates around my little world. A world I once thought was totally mine and the most important little chunk of sunlit wonder under the sun. Now I look back and understand the term accomplishment, and the term egocentric as it makes even me feel small.

I had avoided the war, now called the Civil War, because of my—what I then thought—elevated stature and worth in and to the world, and of course with my father's political influence. I considered myself somewhat a gift to humanity. My father, God bless his departed rotten soul, was a grain merchant. A merchant who became one of Chicago's biggest traders of not only grain but one of the biggest meat merchants in what was now a land united, states and territories, from the Atlantic to the Pacific, from Canada to Florida. United once again now that the South is defeated.

My father, Horatio Augustus Thornton—Gus to his few friends—died peacefully in his sleep. Which was a surprise to me as he had enemies from one ocean to the other. He'd been shot twice, each time by an assassin who claimed he'd been cheated. It seems, and I've concluded, my father never let an honest act stand in the way of profit.

His business was now mine, probably only because he'd never found time to will it away, as he and I had often been at odds.

Both assassins had met their fate at the hands of Samuel Jefferson, a very large, exceptionally strong, man of color who'd escaped from the South. A man who, although graying, was still a force of nature. A man whose services I'd inherited and who now served me.

My father was born as poor as a man can be, thrown onto the rough streets of Chi-town as the ruffians on her streets called her, at the age of seven as his parents, my grandparents, both died early. Grandma, of consumption, as tuberculosis is known, and the more plebeian consumption of demon rum. My grandfather, stumbling drunk it seems, was run over by a two-ton wagon loaded with beer kegs. Both inauspicious ways to depart the earth, but equally effective when it comes to giving up the ghost. And my grandfather's demise in a manner that haunts me at the moment.

To my father's credit, at that ripe old age, he found a way to survive. With a canvas sack, he roamed the feed yards where cattle awaited the slaughterhouse, collecting spilled grain, oft times merely a grain at a time. When he had half a sack full—a story he enjoyed relating to me—he would carry it across town and sell his precious load for a few pennies to a sympathetic hostler who, it seems, admired his spunk. My father, as he described, but only to me, by hook and crook built an empire beginning with those few grains.

So, I was born, or so I was told, to Horatio and Florence Thornton with a proverbial silver spoon in my mouth. Due to my mother's insistence, educated in the best schools, clothed by the finest tailors, trained to fence, shoot, dance, and converse by the finest, I was—I guess am—the epitome of a gentleman. The polar opposite of my father.

Which is part of the reason I now stand in awe studying the features of the wretch before me. I fear it's as if staring into a looking glass. I'd never have come to that conclusion had my coach, traveling possibly a mite too fast down Mission Street in San Francisco, not run him down—the reason I'm a bit haunted by my grandfather's demise. Unlike my father would have done, Samuel, my driver, personal servant, bodyguard, and I gathered the man up and hauled him to the recently completed San Francisco City and County Hospital, where a broken chinbone was set.

Left him bloodied, disheveled, unclean, bearded, head of hair bushy and shoulder length and probably nit filled, in their good care. I presented his caregivers with a twenty-dollar gold coin from my pocket. My guilt was somewhat assuaged until Samuel informed me the man, who'd mumbled his name as Ohio Jones, would be turned out on the street as soon as he was treated.

After the meeting which we finally managed to attend and was the cause of our speeding down Mission Street at a lope, which resulted in the accident, I concluded I must return and assure myself this Ohio fellow was not cast out to starve on San Francisco's rough streets. I did so reluctantly.

Not only had the hospital set his leg, but they'd bathed, shaved, shampooed, and pulled his hair back tied behind his head. And exposed his true appearance.

Now, who the hell, what the hell is this reflection of myself

I stare at, gobsmacked? Other than a scar on his chin and a surly manner, he is me. Samuel, who stands slightly behind me, is open-mouthed as I turn to him.

"What the hell?" I question my black employee, whose wide eyes shine in astonishment equal to my own.

He merely shrugs, then offers, "Maybe de good Lord done ran out of faces and had to start over."

Ohio Jones is on his back, still in a recovery bed, staring at me with equal astonishment and some anger, and finally offers, "You got a bit more fat under them fancy duds, but by God were it not for that I'd say you done stole my face. You'd be a usurper of note."

I collect myself enough to ask. "When are you to be released?"

"Chucked out y'all mean?" His statement is more of a growl than a murmur. "They said they be in need of the bed, so they'll soon bring me a pair of crutches, a gift of the Sisters of Mercy, and throw me out, maybe this very evening... morning at the latest...a gift of these merciless sons a bitch."

Working around the stockyards and slaughterhouses most of my life, such language does not offend me although it is a sign of ignorance, so I overlook it and offer, "I have another must-attend meeting this evening at my hotel, the new Nucleus. Come there and I'll stand you to a late supper—"

"Ha," he snaps angrily. "You're about as swift as a slug. What the hell you think? I'm gonna call my coach to swoop me over to join you? It would take me all night to hobble that far, should the brigands not steal my crutches before I get a block."

I'm a little taken aback, but he's right. "I'll have Samuel here at the front doors this evening, say six, to see if you've been released. If not, again in the morning. We need to talk."

"You mean that same coach done run me down like a lowly cur in the street?"

I'm tempted to say he looks like a cur in the street but

restrain myself. "I mean the coach you, I presume in your cups, stumbled in front of and who we couldn't avoid...yes, that coach."

He merely nods, still with a little fire in his eyes, so I give him my back and we take our leave.

2

I OFTEN RIDE IN THE REAR-FACING SEAT WITH MY BACK TO THE driver as I like to converse with Samuel as we roll along, and this rental coach, like my Brewster back in Chicago, although not as luxurious, has a small slider to speak to the driver. Samuel has become my best friend. That said, I still have to pry his honest thoughts from him.

So, as we return to the Nucleus, after some careful introspection, I open the little slider. "Was I dreaming?" I ask.

He shifts to the side to be better heard. "If'n you was, we done had the same dream. Ain't likely."

"Isn't," I correct, an effort to correct his grammar that has become a game with us over the year I've inherited him as an employee.

"Not where I hail from," he admonishes me, and the game continues.

"God doesn't make two faces exactly alike, as the versions are inestimable."

"If that mean's what I done believe it means, you is right."

"Are right," I correct but he ignores, so I continue. "I want you to bring him to the hotel, be it supper or breakfast, and join us—"

He laughs. "Them hotel folks ain't that open-minded. They'll throw us out. Ain't no man of color never ate in that restaurant."

"I have a suite costing twenty dollars a night and business isn't so good they can pass that up. Besides, I told them you were a Nubian prince and own a diamond mine in Hopetown on the Orange River."

That gets a guffaw from Samuel. "Dang if that ain't a big imagine. You ain't lost your sense of humor."

I laugh as well, then add, "Diamonds impress everyone. *Maximum in rebus humanis, non solum inter gemmas, pretium habet adamas.*"

I sense he's shaking his head, as he always does when I'm showing off my knowledge of languages, particularly Latin. So, I translate without being asked. "Among all human things, not only among gems, the diamond is the most precious."

He replies. "Can't eat it, ain't much of a tool lessin' you want's to scratch sometin'. A pretty babble is all 'tis."

"So, you say. The management of the Nucleus thinks otherwise, so you'll be allowed to join me at my table."

"You white folks are a strange lot," he mumbles.

I laugh, and concur, "As are blacks, yellows, browns, and red men, and many other critters in the animal kingdom."

We ride in silence the rest of the way to the hotel, pull the carriage into a nearby livery, and walk the block, side by side, to the hotel. As he has done before, the doorman tips his hat and stares in wonder as we ascend the stairs and I hold the door for Samuel.

I may be egocentric, but I consider Samuel my friend who was ofttimes my father's savior. I'm learning as I grow older, friendship starts from the heart out and the skin is the last thing of which to be concerned, no matter how others stare, both black and white. Another thing of which I no longer have to worry about disagreeing with my father.

I have an early meeting a few blocks away with rancher and slaughterhouse proprietor Henry Miller, the West's leading cattleman if one considers both raising and slaughtering. Like my father, Miller started at the bottom, Miller as a butcher, and due to the demand for beef and lack of cattle became a rancher. He and his partner, a lawyer named Lux, are interesting fellows, and now with the railroad, prime cuts can be shipped on ice as far as the East Coast and they are particularly interesting to Thornton Holdings.

I spend the rest of the day engrossed in reading and do so until Samuel appears at six thirty with Ohio Jones in tow. I realize as I descend to the hotel sitting room that he's now again attired in his soiled and bloodied canvas pants, blood-covered brogans, and linsey-woolsey shirt that's seen much better days.

Even as the occupant of the hotel's biggest accommodations, the manager looks askance at me, and inquires, "Not in our dining room, please."

I wonder if it's Ohio or Samuel he objects to, or maybe both? But I acquiesce, "Perhaps a private room on this floor? As you can see stairs are out of the question."

He thinks a moment, then offers, "I don't suppose you could eat in our storeroom?" He seems embarrassed to suggest it but adds. "It's clean and organized."

"We'll wait in the lobby until you set up."

"Only a moment or so." I know he'll hurry as he doesn't want us seen, even in the lobby.

Ohio has not said a word since entering, staring at the surroundings as if he's never seen crystal chandeliers, patterned wallpaper, or Chinese carpets. He remains silent as the manager returns, leads us through a side door, down a hallway lined with shelves of linens, blankets, trays and crockery, out into the kitchen, then into a storeroom where a table is set for three.

"Another chair, please?" I request, as I'm sure the leg would be better elevated.

"Another place setting?" the manager asks.

"No, to elevate the leg."

Ohio digs a small bottle out of his torn pants pocket and holds it up to me. "Laudanum, pain-free as long as it lasts."

"Still better elevated," I say, and get a small and almost thankful nod in return.

I pick up the menu and glance at him as he does not do so.

He sees the glance, and offers, "You order. Ain't used to such a place and don't read so good."

I don't need the menu so ask, "Bring us a bottle of your finest wine—"

"Whiskey," Ohio corrects.

"Bring us a bottle of wine and a bottle of San Pablo Rye, three fat loin steaks, medium rare—"

"Mine burnt, please," Ohio says, and I'm surprised with the civility of a please.

"Some of those greens and some potatoes, baked—"

"Fry mine, please," Ohio corrects.

I nod and the manager disappears. Samuel is smiling and gives me a nod.

It's discovery time, so I ask. "Mr. Jones, spin me a tale about yourself. As are you, I'm surprised if we're not related."

"Come here from Ohio," he says.

"Which I presume is why you're so named?"

"That, and I hate my given name."

"Which is?"

"Bartholomew. And I dislike Bart. Ohio ranges wide and free which I admire. You've yet to offer up your'n?"

"Thomas Augustus Thornton, Thom to my friends and I hope you're one. How about your parents?"

"Pa was a butcher, as was his pa. They come from

Germany when he was a sprout. Landed in New York then Chicago, where I was born. Then he come by some money and we lit out to Ohio, or so my ma telled me. I was barely more'n a stain on Pa's long johns when we set out."

Born in Chicago? So, I ask, "And your age?"

"Thirty-four, born the fourteen day of August."

3

THERE'S NO QUESTION IN MY MIND, I'M LOOKING AT A TWIN brother I had no idea I had, but I charge on.

"Nothing about cousins or such?" I ask.

"No. Pa had brothers but them still in Germany. Ma was an orphan."

"So, you still have no idea why you've got my face."

He smiles for the first time. "I kinda figured you had mine."

"Point of view, I guess. So, no idea?"

He ponders a minute, then offers, "Ma said I was a twin, another boy, a couple of minutes older, but he died in childbirth."

"The hell you say. What if he didn't? What if I'm that twin?" I almost choke suggesting it. I'm half a head shorter than my father, and both my parents are fair with blue eyes while mine are ebony black and my hair dark but with wine red highlights as Ohio's is colored. An uncommon color. Could it be?

My mother is still alive and living in New York City, where she escaped when I was only sixteen after many years of abuse from my father. As I was an only child and away at Highland Military School in Worchester, Massachusetts, I never felt deprived or that she left me and, in fact, was happy for her leaving.

Now I have another reason to visit, and that's to find out who I really am.

Even without her confessions, I'm convinced Ohio Jones is my twin brother. No one could possibly have exactly the same features. Monozygotic I believe is the term, only recently surmised by scientists as two in the same embryo, from a single egg that splits.

But it seems features may be the only commonality. He's as rough as I'm refined, as uncouth as I'm couth. And I have to wonder, as dishonest as I am honest?

So, with a ninety percent belief we are twin brothers, I continue my inquiry as he picks at his steak.

"You don't like the beef."

"Damn laudanum has me off my feed. If'n I can't get this down, suppose I wrap it up and take it—"

"Take it where? You have accommodations here in the city?"

He eyes me. "I been sleeping under the stars most my days. I got me a spot in the cypress woods, up near the Presidio. I got my bedroll and Sharps hid out there with a few silver pieces since I sold my horse and mule. Colt is enough." He pats the revolver on his hip.

I have to ask, "So, you came horseback all the way from Ohio?"

"Nope. Had me a few dollars from selling the farm and rode a side-wheeler down the Ohio, up the Mississippi, on up the Missouri to Fort Benton, and horsebacked from there. Backtracked a little to the Bozeman Trail south to the California Trail. Killed me a couple of buffalo, a couple of elk, a few deer, and a couple of Indians who wanted my hair. All in all, a fine trip."

"You sell any other items?"

"Nope. Like I done said, got my Sharps hid out with my bedroll and I'm pleased to report them nurses didn't filch my Colt or my belly-gun, which is even now in the boot on my good foot."

I ponder that a moment, then suggest, "No need to hurry that steak. If you'd accept, I'd like Samuel to give you a lift to recover your belongings and put you up here at the hotel. I do believe we have much to talk about."

For the first time since the hospital, I see the hackles raise on his neck, and he eyes me with that fire. "Brother or no, twin or no, I ain't no charity case. I carry my own weight, even on a broke hind leg. I figured you owed me this hunk of beef, but now we're even."

"I owe you much more for breaking that hind leg as you call it. A couple of days room and board at least."

"I'm beholdin' to no man and won't be."

So, I turn to Samuel. "How about it, Samuel. You're the fairest man I know. You think I owe Mr. Jones here a few days room and board."

He smiles and turns to Ohio. "Mr. Jones, you gonna look this gift horse in the mouth?"

"Beholdin' to no man," Ohio growls.

"How about I break the other leg to help you come to your senses?" Samuel asks, but with a smile.

Ohio glares at him a moment, before he growls back, "Darky, I put more than one man flat on his back who tested my sand, and I believe—"

"Two days," I interrupt. "That's not too much to ask of a brother who neither of us knew we had for thirty-four years."

He's quiet for a moment, then finally speaks, "Don't mean I owe you a damn thing."

"Not a farthing," I say.

He half smiles. "What the hell's a farthing?"

And I laugh. "Doesn't matter since you won't owe me that

or anything else. But a little conversation along the way won't hurt either of us."

He eyes us both, back and forth, then relents. "Must be the damn laudanum, but two nights will do."

We arrange for his room, he and Samuel head out to retrieve his personals, and I retire to the men's smoking and game room where two tables are engaged in cards. One of draw poker, the other four playing partners cribbage, trading off each game with the fellow on the left then the right.

I set in on the poker table, more for the conversation than the game. I introduce myself to the four at the table, one a drummer selling agricultural equipment, one a banker with Wells Fargo and Company, one a sailing captain just in from the Sandwich Islands, and one a police captain up from the bustling town of Los Angeles. I'm barely seated and dealt the first hand when the police captain begins firing questions at me.

I'm finally getting a little irritated with the man's inquisition and brace him. "You, sir, seem overly interested in myself. May I ask why?"

"Well, sir, I don't believe a word you sprout..." He pulls a folded flyer from his waistcoat pocket and spreads it on the table, then asks the others, "Gentlemen, am I wrong or does Mr. Thornton here share a remarkable likeness with this gentleman on this freshly printed flyer? A gentleman who robbed Johnny Jackson's Saloon and Sporting House just yesterday and left his bartender bleeding on the floor."

I stare at the flyer, pick it up and stare some more, and don't notice the police captain's firearm aimed at my heart until I replace it flat on the table.

Never taking his eyes off me, he says, "Sorry, gentlemen, but I have to cash in. Mr. Thornton and I need to stroll down to police headquarters and see what the city marshal wants to do with him."

I was rather excited about having a twin brother, now I'm even more so, if excited, apprehensive, and angry to the bone marrow means the same thing.

4

FIVE HOURS AGO, I WOULD HAVE GIVEN YOU A THOUSAND-TO-ONE
odds that I'd never see the inside of a jail cell...now, thank
God for small favors, I'm in a private one but sandwiched
between one holding five Sydney Duck gang members and
one with a pair of Californios, Mexican heritage. The jailer has
taken my pocket watch and other personals, so I have no idea
the time or how long I've tossed and turned.

A whisper of light is beginning to appear over the East
Bay. To be truthful, I haven't slept a wink and with every
moment I'm more astounded I'm here, and equally that
Samuel has not appeared with San Francisco's finest lawyer
in tow to show the city marshal the error of his ways. City
Marshal O'Brien, a fellow of generous girth and a loud
manner who seems jubilant to have a well-dressed gentleman
as a guest in his gray stone manor.

Thoughts have raced through my mind faster than the
Transcontinental rambles over the track. The worst of them
wondering if Samuel has not been murdered and pilfered by
my newly discovered twin brother. Only hours ago, I felt
blessed to discover Ohio, even though he's a ruffian and we

seem to be at the utter ends of the social ladder. Now I rue the moment he stepped in front of my coach and even wonder if the lout didn't do so purposely to gain the favor and care of a man who could afford such a conveyance.

My worst thought is he has murdered my good friend and body servant Samuel.

Finding my twin? Not a blessing but a curse. Hours ago, I was the finest gentleman imaginable, now I'm conjuring how to murder my twin brother.

And wondering if I'm to meet my maker after having my neck snapped at the end of a hemp rope, knotted with the thirteen turns of the hangman. Fate strikes like the tip of a coachman's whip.

Something rattles at my cell door and I open my eyes, sure I'll see Samuel's smile and the jailor with an apologetic look and key in hand, but rather it's a wheeled cart carrying a pair of buckets out of which he ladles a cup of water and from the other a cup of gruel.

"Well, boyo," he says with a crooked grin, "you done graduated?"

"How so?" I ask, with both hope and apprehension.

"Johnny Jackson's bartender, Mace McToon, done went to meet his maker in the night?"

"I know no Mace McToon, so how does that concern me?"

Again, I get the crooked smile. "Well, boyo, he's the bartender you robbed and shot yesterday. So now the charge ain't merely robbery and assault, now it's a hanging offense. Murder, and we got a hanging judge on the bench. Your neck is gonna stretch."

He guffaws like a hyena as he moves on to the Californio's cell.

Trying to ignore the threat, knowing how wrong he must be, I return to eyeing my bowl. Yesterday my breakfast was two perfectly poached eggs atop a divinely toasted slice of brioche, half a peach covered with thickened sweet cream, a cup of French-brewed coffee, and a glass of juice from oranges. Which I enjoyed probably as much as the weevils I see doing the breaststroke in the runny gruel are enjoying their swim and feast.

I'm hungry, but not hungry enough to pass this horrid mess over my lip.

One of the Sydney Ducks sidles up to the bars separating our cells, and asks, "So, fancy Dan, you ain't gonna eat your breakfast?"

Not the least bit interested in engaging in a conversation with the lout I merely shake my head and hand him my bowl through the bars.

He takes it and nods. "Obliged, mate."

I merely nod back, but he continues. "You'd be a man of means, then?"

"I'm comfortable enough," I reply, thinking it rude not to do so.

I hand him a calling card…then almost snatch it back realizing how stupid it must be.

He takes it, gives me a nod, then comments with a wandering glance from my well-shined brogans to my dollar haircut, then guffaws and comments, "Damn if you don't smell as sweet as a Cajun whore. Too damn bad you ain't over here where we could show you the use of one."

All five of them slap their thighs and crow like roosters. I do not find his comment amusing.

At midmorning Samuel appears in the company of a guard. And to my great surprise, Ohio clomps along on crutches at their side.

Would Ohio appear if he was guilty of robbery and murder?

Samuel, seeing my look of both apprehension and relief, starts explaining before they reach my cell.

"Johnny Jackson, who owns the saloon what was robbed and who employed the bartender shot, saw the killer close as you and me, and was here when we appeared. A couple of confused coppers grabbed on to Ohio and relieved him of his fine Sharps rifle and his sidearm, and me of my little belly-gun and treated us both badly until this Jackson gent stepped forward and yelled at them to hold up."

"And?" I ask.

"And he done said the robber was a half head taller than Ohio and didn't have no scar on his chin. We still got to see the judge, but it seems we pay some bail and get out until this is settled."

"Why the judge?"

Samuel's eyes drop to the floor, seemingly embarrassed, and it's his turn to mumble. "Seems I knocked the tooth outta one of them coppers, and Ohio here made another lose his breakfast by whackin' him in his egg pouch with his crutch."

I have to chuckle.

"Town marshal, fellow named O'Brien, saw it all and chastised his coppers for being hasty and a mite rough. Still, we all have to appear to see what Judge McGillicutty has to say."

"Thank God," I mumble, then address Ohio. "I apologize for thinking badly of you, brother. You've proved to be a stand-up fellow by coming down here at the risk of this jail cell."

He clears his throat before replying. "Well, brother, if that's what we're to call each other. I may not be your idea of the brother you'd like to have, but I ain't told a lie since I pocketed me a piece of candy from the Canton, Ohio, general store near thirty years ago."

I nod. "That's my idea of a brother. Maybe we can finally talk after this chat with the judge."

He's quiet for a moment as we head down the hall, then

stops me before we exit the jail cells. "You know, brother. I'm not sure it's to my liking having another fellow looking exactly like me, so if it's all the same to you, I believe I'll take my leave of you and this damnable. I ain't gonna leave nothing but tracks and get to where the air's clean and I ain't smelling crabs boiling or garbage in the streets."

5

JUDGE MCGILLICUTTY SPEAKS WITH A BIT OF AN ENGLISH ACCENT tinged with Scots Highland, with a demeanor even more officious than most. His porkchop sideburns extend two inches beyond his ears and damn near to the jawline. He enjoys rapping his gavel and it's a good thing his high desk is made of solid oak. Constantly smoking a long-stemmed pipe. He enjoys knocking the dottle out of it as loudly as banging his echoing gavel. He does not take lightly police officers being assaulted even though City Marshal O'Brien, the coppers' boss, testifies that his men acted hastily, and that Ohio and Samuel merely defended themselves.

I'm happy to walk away with a fifty-dollar fine payable to the court plus ten dollars to the copper who lost a tooth. The one kicked in the nut sack is walking without a limp so he goes unrewarded, although he may never father another child. He claimed bruising and swelling, but is reluctant to display the evidence and the judge does not insist.

As we mount the coach after court, Ohio asks, "How about taking me back to my Cypress forest. I'll lay low there until this chinbone heals—"

"You got twenty-seven and a half dollars," I snap. The fact

is I care little about the money, in fact nothing. What I do care about is Ohio hanging around long enough for us to really get to know each other. An aspiration he obviously doesn't share.

"What business is that of yours, brother or not?"

"You owe me half that fine I paid."

"I got six dollars and seventy-nine cents last count. I guess you'd take my last dollar?"

"You claim to be an honorable man, so I'll let you work it off. Say a dollar a day and I'll throw in room and board."

He eyes me carefully. "You got me, but that don't make you much more than a son of a bitch and don't mean I have to spill my life story."

I have to laugh. "As we seem to share the same mother, are you sure that's the expletive you want to use?"

"What the hell's an expletive?"

"Curse."

That seems to set him back on his heels. Then he tries to cover a hard smile. "So, I guess bastard ain't much better?"

"Not much."

"What do I do for this dollar a day and found?"

"You fill in for Samuel should I send him on an errand or back him up should we be in a compromising situation."

He spits in his palm and extends his hand to shake. For the first time in my thirty-four years, I follow suit, then without thinking remove my hanky from a rear pocket and mop my hand.

He finds that funny and laughs. His laugh is infectious and both Samuel and I follow suit. I think it's only partially because of the spit in the hand, more likely because all of us are not lolling away in a cold jail cell. We all laugh until out of breath.

We're on our way back to the Nucleus when I spot a haberdashery and yell through the slot for Samuel to pull up. Even before we dismount the coach, Ohio complains, "I got no funds for fancy duds."

I reply, "First, they won't be fancy, second, they won't be yours. They'll be mine and you'll be expected to wear them like a uniform."

He seems to accept that, and we leave Goldman's with a brush and soap mug, razor, tortoise comb, and Ohio wearing decent gray wool trousers, white cotton shirt, four-in-hand tie, matching coat, waistcoat, and black brogans...and carrying a linen sack holding a second shirt, dark brown trousers, and seconds for everything but the brogans.

We are back at the hotel in time for lunch. I recently read a copy of the *Alta California* and an article proclaiming "The first carload of Baltimore and New York oysters in shells, cans, kegs, all in splendid order, has arrived, packed and shipped by the pioneer oyster house of the west, A. Booth, Chicago, Ill."

I'm long an aficionado of oysters and it seems I'll not have to leave the treat behind in Chicago. They've long been in the West but those dredged from San Francisco and San Pablo Bay are not large. The Transcontinental has designed and built aquarium cars and now brings oysters and spat west. They have been seeding the bay in private beds so soon the city will enjoy large eastern oysters dredged as close and fresh as a view outside its windows.

The next few days, along with meetings with prominent parties of the West that will benefit Thornton Holdings, I'm having a great time even if acting aloof of the whole process, introducing my twin to the comforts of fortune.

Ohio's soon consuming oysters like an Astor, wearing ready-to-wear and polished brogans as if born to them. He complains his belly-gun won't fit in his brogans but accepts a small holster that cradles in the center of his back. He accepts it as I insist it part of his job is backing up Samuel as my bodyguard.

I'm also amused to observe folks glancing back and forth, then back and forth again as they realize there are two of me, some who have known me for the short time I've been in the West must wonder if I've separated, split like an amoeba?

It's been a week and my and Samuel's relationship with my brother continues to deepen, as I'd hoped. As talk is among the cheapest commodities on earth, I'm sure as a pilgrim who's crossed the great unknown, faced grizzly bears, Indians, unspeakable weather, and other maladies he'd be little impressed with my exploits. He still thinks of me as a dandy and still would if, with seeming braggadocio, I related the fact I'd faced many insulting opponents in the stockyards with fists, fought one duel with pistols and prevailed, could ride my mount over a six-foot rail and have done so many times. Only time and circumstance will demonstrate that under my well-tailored attire I'm fairly fearless.

It's the sixth night since Ohio has shared a hotel if not a room when a sound knock awakens me. It's too dark to read my pocket watch so I have no idea what time it might be. I stumble to the door in my nightshirt and having seen my father shot when opening a door, I'm cautious.

"State your business?" I raise my voice.

"Mr. Thornton, sorry to bother but we're vacating. We have a fire in the kitchen."

That rocks me and I snatch the door open. Only as I see the club descending do I realize I recognize the Australian accent.

I get a glance at the ceiling as I'm going to my back on the plush Chinese rug.

6

AWAKING WITH A RIP-ROARING HEADACHE, IN THE DARKNESS, I try to set up but jerk against hemp ropes binding me securely to the planks beneath. And I'm cold, realizing I'm still bare-legged in my nightshirt. The smells of a filthy bilge should have apprised me my location as soon as my eyes opened, but when one's head feels as it's been used to pile-drive posts it takes a moment to assemble sound, motion, and smell.

"Hello," I say, then raise my voice. "Hello!" Then shout, "Where the hell am I?"

I hear footfalls on planks, then a door or hatch opens, and morning light floods the small cabin I occupy. A body fills the opening, the light behind the figure so I can't recognize the face, and a gruff voice with that same Australian accent admonishes me.

"Shut up, we ain't cleared the harbor yet."

I'm silent a moment, then yell, "I have no interest in clearing the harbor. HELP!"

He's on me in a heartbeat, covering my mouth with a large, calloused hand stinking of sea life. "Shut yer pie hole, mate."

Again, I'm silent, then nod my head and he removes his paw.

"Who the hell are you and where the hell am I?" I growl.

"We done met, mate. You be the fancy Dan in the cell next to me and my mates."

"I gave you my breakfast."

"That club didn't knock all the sense from your noggin. You are the guest of the Mission Street Ducks and will be home safe soon as your mates deliver five thousand to me and mine."

"So, I'm being held for ransom?"

"Call it what you may." He chuckles. "I'd be saying it's payment for this little cruise around the bay."

I absorb that a moment before being sarcastic. "Well, mate, I don't remember booking a cruise."

"You'll be working while aboard. You ever seen an oyster dredger?"

I'd smile if I didn't hurt so badly as oysters had recently been the subject of conversation. "Seen, but never been aboard? No. How about loosening these ropes—"

"Lines, when aboard a sailing vessel, mate."

"Whatever you call them, how about loosening them?"

"When we're a good distance from the harbor. They be five of us aboard and it be too damn far to swim, you'll have a coffee, a bowl of chowder, then a spell at the drag to earn yer keep. Don't make me draw this Colt on my hip. I draw it, I use it."

So, again, I nod. And he gives me his back and retreats up the ladder.

It may come as a surprise to my hosts, but I know a line from a rope, a foremast from a mizzen, a mainsail from a jib. My father had a fifty-foot ketch and we often sailed Lake Michigan. But it's a fact I'll keep to myself.

It's another few minutes before my captor returns.

"Should I let you up, you gonna be a nice, polite dandy?" he asks.

"Must be four or five aboard. What's a dandy to do against those odds?"

"Your fellows will deliver the money even if we have to deep-six you, so I'd be mindful of that."

"My pleasure to work for my keep," I lie. "So, you bet. Loosen these lines and find me some trousers and brogans."

"You learn fast for a soft-handed dandy." And he does. I rub my wrists and ankles before swinging my legs over. He hands me a mug of cold chowder, clams I'd guess, and I down it in a few gulps and chews.

"You ready to topside?" he asks when I finish, handing me some trousers and a pair of beat-up brogans. I'm sure I'm a sight with nightshirt over filthy canvas trousers, and it hanging to my knees, and brogans with a hole in the toe and no stockings.

"Let's go to work," I snap. "Anything is better than this stink hole. You got a name?"

"Sticker will do for you. And you give me grief and you'll learn why." He pats a long Arkansas toothpick in a sheath on his belt. Then adds, "and it could be Shooter," and pats the Colt on the other side.

He laughs and pushes me ahead and I step out onto the deck of a forty-foot oyster dredger and see four men hard at work. She's a ketch-rigged vessel but is square across the stern where rigged with a geared wheel and a claw. In the morning light I recognize my captor as the man who'd clubbed me at my hotel door.

He shouts and all turn to face me. "Mates," he yells, "this is our new hand. You can call him Dandy Dan."

The oldest of the five, a man with one eye glazed the color of the inside of an oyster shell, strides over but doesn't extend a hand. He eyes me up and down and turns to Sticker. "He'll work or he don't eat."

Sticker laughs, then introduces the others. "This be Capt'n Jack, that's Rooster, Toby, and Robin. We'll be at the East Bay beds in a few minutes and will dredge a while then y'all will haul the take aboard. We'll only be a quarter mile from shore, oft times less, but don't think you can swim it. There be a six- or seven-knot current when the tides coming in or out, and you'll be swept out to sea to feed the sharks you try."

"I can't swim," I lie again. I swim like a porpoise. But I'll bide my time.

Sticker continues to instruct me. "There may be a bay copper or two, patrol boat, come alongside. They be looking for oyster pirates—"

"Oyster pirates?" I ask.

"Oyster beds out here are private, claimed by dudes like you. Maintained and guarded by them what claim to own them. Come dark, others steal with quick sweeps in and away. So private coppers are hired by them what own the beds, and they check boats on occasion."

I shrug.

"You yell out and them boys will go to Davy Jones's locker. I got a double-barrel Coach gun loaded with cut up square nails. And I got no problem unloading it on bay coppers or you, so don't test me."

I merely nod, and eye the distant shore wondering if I can make that swim before being caught.

7

AT ONE TIME MY HANDS WERE HARD FROM WORKING THE YARDS, earning the title cowpoke as I started with a pole in hand, moving the critters into line and along into the slaughterhouse.

But I soon learn, as I join in to turn the crank to pull up the dredge, that hard hands are only a memory. By the mid-time of the second pull of the dredge, my palms and fingers are forming nice blisters.

The dredge is dumped on deck, the oysters and occasional clam is sorted out, then the trash is shoved through scuppers back to rejoin the bay floor.

Robin is a young fella, in his teens I'd guess, and he takes pity on me and fetches some bacon grease from the larder which soothes the blisters somewhat. Still, by the time the day sees the sun dropping into the pass that opens the bay to the Pacific, my hands are bleeding from broken blisters.

I am not surprised when Capt'n Jack works the ketch nearer and nearer a long pier coming offshore from Oakland, a settlement on the east shore. A structure on the end of that pier is explained by Robin to be an oyster house, where the shellfish are shucked and where guards watch out for pirates. These oyster beds are claimed by private owners.

"Are we pirates?" I ask Robin.

He laughs, then offers, "Not until it's dead dark, and only then if it be a narrow moon and dark night."

Almost as soon as I say it, I see a skiff being manned alongside the pier, and soon two men are handling the oars, with another in the bow standing with scatter-gun in hand.

Sticker moves over alongside me. "Remember my scatter-gun, Dandy. You yell out and them fellas is crab food along with you."

"You kill me, and my fellas won't pay up," I admonish.

"They won't know you be toes up and will pay up. So, keep your lip buttoned."

"Hell, Sticker, I'm having such a good time blister'n up my hands why would I want to leave?"

That gets a chuckle out of him. He moves to the ladder and digs out a key out of his pocket and opens a closet and pulls out a double-barrel scatter-gun as the skiff gets within shouting, and shooting, range.

A broad-chested lout in the bow of the skiff yells out, "Coming alongside," and Sticker hands the shotgun to Capt'n Jack, who leans on the rail, making sure they see he's armed.

Jack shouts back. "You can come closer, but if'n you try to board they'll be hell to pay."

Only then do I realize Jack has a Sydney Duck accent as well. I wondered if he'd merely been hired to take Sticker and me aboard, now I figure he's part of the plot.

They row up to within twenty feet and the two on the oars have to continue to row as we're moving along at three knots or so.

"You're too close to the Ocean Glory beds. Keep your distance!" broad-chested shouts.

"Bugger you. I'm well clear," Jack snaps.

"You're too damn close. My man in the tower yonder has a Sharps and he'll damn sure hole you just below the water-line, you get any closer."

"And should he make such a reckless act I'll uncover the four-pound cannon I got forward and make splinters outta your house and pier."

"Your stern says you're the *Misty Ann*; I'll note that and be on the watch for you."

I haven't been told the name of my host's boat, but now I know. Old broad-chest turns to me. "Hey, sleepy, you just crawl outta your bunk?" I don't answer so he continues. "Didn't I see you near the Silver Slipper this morning in city duds?"

"Wasn't me, mate," I answer, wondering if it was Ohio he saw.

"Keep your distance," the man in the skiff yells back, turning his attention again to the captain. "You won't be warned next time."

"Bugger off, boyo," Jack says, and they row away.

I turn to Sticker. "Good enough?"

"Yep. Now, get your blistered butt back to work."

By sundown we've rounded a point to be out of sight of the oyster house and dropped anchor. We do have another bowl of chowder. The chowder's been freshened with the fish caught in the dredge.

After we finish Jack instructs us, "Hit the deck, boys, now to pay for this little sojourn."

We crank the capstan and haul anchor. The tide has turned and now we have its help going the opposite direction. We've been traveling south, away from the Sacramento River which I'd ridden to San Francisco. Now it is north, toward the river's confluence with the bay, riding the tide.

As we round the point, young Robin comes to my side. "Should you hear a gunshot, hit the deck."

I nod, then ask, "We're headed to dredge that private bed?"

"We are."

Glancing up I see we have nearly half a moon.

"Pretty damn light," I suggest.

"Too damn light. But we're headed to Yerba Buena Island soon as we make two or three passes. I heared Capt'n Jack and Sticker jabberin'. Seems they be a meeting with friends of your'n scheduled for there."

"Then," I can't help but caution, "it should be you ready to duck if you hear gunshots."

"You should know, Mr. Dandy—"

"Name is Thornton. Thom Thornton."

"Mr. Thornton, I ain't part of this whatever it is with you. I'm hired on as an oysterman and that's the width and depth of it. I hope you're to fare well in all this."

Sticker's voice rings across the deck. "What the hell is the conflab all about. Get to work."

"Makin' small talk," Robin replies, and strides away.

To hell with his "get to work." I stand looking out over the water, judging the darkness and the distance from where I'm sure we'll dredge at the edge of the private bed, to the oyster house and pier...and safety. A try for the pier seems in order. I'll be hard to spot in the darkness.

A crushing blow to my kidneys drops me to my knees.

"I done telled you to go to work, now work it is," Capt'n Jack seems to have taken umbrage with me enjoying the moonlit night. He's driven the scatter-gun's butt, what feels to be four inches, deep into my lower back and left kidney. The pain is intense and I'm wondering if I can walk, much less swim. I stumble to the dredge crank and take up a position facing young Robin.

"Dredge away," Jack says, and we loose the crank to spin freely. "Hold there," Jack instructs when the dredge crank slows to match the speed of the boat, obviously reaching bottom and the oyster bed. As always happens, the ketch jerks and slows when the metal forks dig in to the sea bottom.

There's an oil lamp in the small two-man tower atop the oyster house so I can fairly judge the distance as we get as near as I think we will on this pass...I contemplate diving overboard. Capt'n Jack still has the scatter-gun hanging at his side. A major deterrent. I take a step backward away from the crank, and an even bigger deterrent is the fact I almost sink to my knees again. The pain in what I suppose is a bruised kidney is one of the worst to ever rack my backbone.

So, I step forward to grab the crank with both hands, looking as if I'm earnestly going back to work, but in fact trying to hold on to keep from hitting my knees.

"Hit the deck," Robin yells, as a muzzle flash lights the interior of the little tower and a big slug slams into the plank side of the boat.

"Coming about," Capt'n Jack yells and we swing hard starboard away from the oyster house, and Toby and Rooster reset the sails.

"Crank, you worthless soggers," Jack yells, and Robin and I have to regain our feet to begin raising the dredge. It's shallow at the private beds so she's up in short order. We're exposed as the deckhouse is forward, another flash and a big slug slams into the stanchion holding the crank. Robin is on the aft side, he and the stanchion offering some protection to me as I'm forward. He begins sagging to the deck and I wipe my face with the back of my hand...realizing I'm covered with blood, and as he flops to the deck I realize it's Robin's.

I have no interest in stopping one of the big Sharps's slugs and dive to the deck beside Robin. He's lying on his side, staring wide-eyed at me, holding his intestines in with both hands. Had he not been facing the stanchion which kept him on his feet for a moment he'd have been flat on his face on the deck.

"Dandy," he manages aloud, then whispers, "I'm kilt." His eyes flutter and he moves no more.

I hear Capt'n Jack yell at Sticker, "Take the wheel," and see him do so. Carrying the scatter-gun, Jack climbs to his feet I guess now feeling safe as the darkness has closed in behind us.

Climbing to my knees, I'm kneeling beside Robin, feeling the anger creep up my backbone. I guess the captain has little fear of "Dandy" as he walks up beside me, the shotgun hanging at his side between he and I and it's cocked.

Within easy reach.

"Damn," he mutters, "that young'un was a fair hand. Y'all throw him overboard," he says, and that burns me. With one hand I move the muzzle over his foot and with the other cover his hand.

As the roar and gun smoke cover the deck he screams and stumbles away, his foot gone. He's up against the rail. I'm on my feet and follow and using his own momentum shove him. Now I'm carrying the scatter-gun.

I cock the other barrel as I turn to see Sticker charging my way. Charging only momentarily as I fire the second barrel and blow a gut-hole big enough for a seagull to fly through.

The other two hands have retreated forward to keep the deckhouse between them and the oyster house and Sharps.

With the wheel released the ketch turns into the wind and luffs, slowing.

I'm fresh out of firepower but realize that Sticker still has the Colt holstered on his side. I limp over and relieve him of it and turn in time to see Rooster and Toby rounding the deckhouse.

"Both them dead?" Rooster asks, and takes a step toward me.

"No deader than you're gonna be you take another step my way."

He stops short and Toby ducks behind him.

"Move to the larboard side," I command, using the Colt as a pointer.

"What now?" Rooster asks.

"Now we're gonna set sail for this Yerba Buena Island and see if I got friends there. One of you is gonna mind the wheel, the other the sails. I'm gonna set atop the deckhouse and keep an eye on you both."

Toby yells out from behind Rooster. "We was just doin' what was tolt us. We wasn't in on no plot or plan. We are making two dollars the day and three percent of the oyster money and that's all we know."

"Well, sir," I say, "just keep doing what you're told and you won't end up washing the deck with your blood like Jack and Sticker."

It takes us over an hour to reach Yerba Buena Island and I have no idea how we're expected to find Samuel and Ohio and whoever else might be awaiting us. As we near, Rooster calls out. "I heard the Capt'n talking to Sticker. Sticker said at eight bells they'd light a fire and we're to drop anchor." We have to circle the island three times before 4 a.m. comes around, and sure as the tide rises and falls, a fire appears on the San Francisco side. I drop anchor only one hundred feet from the shoreline, which seems very steep there. The outgoing tide keeps the bow pointed south and straining against the anchor rode.

It's only minutes before I hear a voice ring over the waves. "Hello, the boat."

"Hello back," I yell.

"Thom Thornton?" Samuel questions.

"Come aboard, Samuel. We have taken the craft and have two prisoners."

"Prisoners!" Rooster cries out. "Hell, we're just deckhands."

"We'll sort that out later," I say. "You two flop down on your butts and keep your hands raised."

I'm a little surprised that Ohio is nowhere in sight. Then as they throw me a line, Samuel turns in the four-man skiff and I hear, "Come on up, Mr. Jones. Seems Mr. Thornton has things in hand."

A tarp sweeps aside and Ohio, swinging his Sharps back and forth, rises like a phoenix out of the bottom. He's on one knee with his splinted leg pointed forward. I can't help but grin and think of his bravado going into a possible gunfight with a broken leg, balanced on a wavering skiff.

"All's well, gentlemen," I say with a grin. "Welcome aboard."

I move to the rail and between Samuel and I we get Ohio and his Sharps and a cane aboard. He laughs as soon as his good foot is on solid deck, and Samuel alights behind him.

Ohio scans the deck then turns to me, "Damn, I shoulda stayed in that warm room. Seems, brother, you have things in hand. Two men dead, two with raised hands. You been busy."

"And one overboard with a foot blown off, hopefully feeding the sharks. Took me a while, but it seems we have things in hand. However, I'd favor a warm room myself."

Samuel stands with hands on hips, eying the two seated on the deck with their hands in the air, and the dead young man on the deck, and Sticker, who's paid for raising the hen's-egg-size knot on my head. Finally, Ohio shakes his head. "You want I limp over and bind them two live fellows up so we can deliver them to the town marshal?"

As soon as he finishes, I nod, but suggest, "Samuel ties a fine knot." And Samuel turns to the task, but before he can take a step both Rooster and Toby clamor to their feet as if to offer their wrists to be bound, but instead spin and dive overboard.

"What the devil?" Samuel says.

"I can pick 'em off," Ohio offers, and raises the muzzle of the Sharps.

"I do believe the good Lord and San Francisco Bay will

resolve that problem. Based on the tug on the anchor rode I'd guess the tide moving at six or seven knots. They'll never make Yerba Buena Island and it's over twenty miles to the north shore. To hell with them. They'll likely feed the sharks out at the Farallon Islands soon enough." I kneel by Robin's body and lay a hand on his chest above his bloodied wound. "This young man was a stand-up fella. Let's see if he has relations who'd like to learn his fate and his good nature."

As we're sailing back to the harbor, Ohio joins me at the wheel.

"Brother, to be honest, it seems I hurt when you hurt, and I felt every damn moment of your trials and tribulations with these louts. Could that be possible?"

"I've heard," I answer slowly, my eyes remaining on our course and the distant harbor lights of San Francisco, "that there's a strange connection between twins. If you'll hang around long enough, let's see if that's a true thing?"

He smiles. "Don't have anything else on my busy schedule."

We're both silent a moment, then he asks, "What's that Chicago like. Big buildings I hear?"

"Well, brother, you won't smell any crabs boiling. You're on the family payroll long as you care to be, so let's clear this little matter of a dead young man, a dead hooligan, a captain with half a foot hopefully feeding the sharks, and a couple of men overboard headed for the Farallons." I sigh deeply concluding I'm safely on my way back to a warm hotel. So I add, "Time comes we'll ride the rails back that way and you can see for yourself. After we clear things up here."

"That may take a while," Ohio says, with a smile. "I'm beginning to believe there ain't so much different twixt us after all."

"And, since you don't have anything else on your schedule, I'd kinda like to hunt down the fella who shot that bartender and cost me a day in jail where I met some fellas who tried to stiff Thornton Holdings out of five thousand hard-earned and gave me a headache that's still niggling at me."

Ohio nods his head, and adds, "I ain't much with fancy tableware and wines I can't pronounce, but I'm a fair hunter."

"Then, brother, let's go hunting."

Dark Highway

John D. Nesbitt

Dark Highway

A BARE SPOT APPEARED IN THE MIDDLE OF THE BLOCK WHERE I expected to find my old Plymouth. I had walked about ten blocks from the place where my ride left me off on the Esplanade, and I was not tired, but a sense of fatigue came over me. I had been worried about whether the car would start, and now it was gone. I lingered at the empty space for a couple of minutes with my traveling bag at my foot. I concluded that I was going to have to go to the police station, and the day was slipping away, so I set out.

I retraced about eight of the blocks I had just covered and walked another half dozen. The coolness of late afternoon was setting in, and the smell of burning leaves hung in the air. I knew where the police station was, as I had been brought in a few months earlier for failure to appear on a hitchhiking ticket. I went in through the glass door and presented myself at the counter with the plexiglass pane.

A weary-looking, middle-aged man in a khaki uniform and brass nameplate took my question and thumbed through a stack of pages. He said, "That car was impounded because it was abandoned on a city street."

I asked, "Why did someone think it was abandoned?"

He narrowed his eyes at the page and said, "It had a flat tire."

My spirits sank further than before. I said, "I only left it there for a few days when I was out of town picking olives." In reality, I had been gone almost two weeks.

The man gave me a matter-of-fact look and said, "That's the way they do it when a car is left on the street unattended." He wrote on a slip of paper and handed it to me. "Here's where they took it to."

I thanked him and went out into the hazy afternoon. I knew where the junkyard was, out on the south edge of town where the main avenue met the freeway. I did not want to push my luck by hitchhiking in town, so I hoofed it.

I walked past parked cars with bumper stickers for the recent election. Reagan had just been elected governor, a big turnover. That and the Dodgers losing the World Series to the Orioles in four games were the big news events that had come to me when I was working in the fields and staying in cabin courts that fall.

I saw my car from a couple of blocks away, on the other side of a chain link fence in a separate area for impounded cars. Closer, I saw it leaning on the left rear. The car had a sad appearance, dull gray with rusty red primer showing through the hood and roof where the paint had worn. The windshield and round headlights gave a blank stare.

A young fellow not much older than me was listening to Patsy Cline on the radio in the office. I told him I came to see about getting my '53 Plymouth.

He found the bill, wrote on it, and showed it to me. The hope went out of me when I saw the amount of sixty-eight dollars. He explained that the original towing was thirty-five, then three dollars was being added each day for storage.

I had to think. I had paid only sixty dollars for the car and had driven it a month. It would take almost all I had, a little over eighty, to get it out of hock and fix the flat tire, and I was still looking at repairs to see why I had been having trouble starting it.

"I can't do it," I said. "It's more than I've got in it. Do you think I could open the trunk and take a couple of things I need?"

He shook his head. "They won't let us. Sorry."

I thanked him and walked out. I took a backward glance at the tired old Plymouth, locked up in an over-priced storage area. *That's how they do it*, I thought. But I couldn't be too bitter. It was what I had done, or not done, that had caused me to take the loss.

––––––––

AFTER A NIGHT in a cheap hotel and a breakfast of hotcakes and coffee, I was on the street again. I had been brooding all along about the days getting shorter, the weather getting colder and damper, and the work getting scarcer. I had read more than once a letter from a girl named Linda. We had spent a night together and had hit it off, but she went to a town called Vista, down in San Diego County, to stay with her cousin. She wrote me to tell me they were sharing an apartment and both working. The weather was always warm, there was lots of work, and I should visit her.

I thought, I didn't have anything keeping me here. I was going to have to start over at finding work, finding a place to stay, and getting back and forth. I had done it plenty of times, and I could always do it again if I came back. I was unhappy with the way things had turned out with my car, and I didn't want to fritter my money away on cheap hotel rooms and cafés. At least I had a little money to travel on, and the day was starting out warm and dry.

I called Linda's number, and no one answered. I decided I would call later.

By nine that morning, I was standing on the side of

Highway 99E, headed south out of Chico. I went where my rides took me, through Gridley and Live Oak and Yuba City to Sacramento, then over toward the Bay Area and down along the east side, through Walnut Creek, then south to San Jose, Morgan Hill, Gilroy, and Prunedale, a town I had forgotten. I saw fields and orchards in an area where I had worked in recent years, just as I had worked in and around the towns in the Sacramento Valley. Just about all of the crops were in now, and many of the fields and orchards had new green grass with the rains of early fall.

I was not sentimental about any of it. I felt more at home in places like Orland and Chico and Gridley than in Morgan Hill, Gilroy, and Watsonville, but they were all places I could come back to for work if I wanted.

The last in my first series of rides left me off in Salinas, which was no longer open highway but freeway again. I got stuck at a freeway on-ramp, not the first time for me in Salinas, which I felt was a crummy town where people drove by and gave unfriendly looks. I imagined most of them were local residents getting off work who didn't like strangers and wouldn't have taken me very far anyway.

After what seemed like a long time, a fellow in a dark-blue-and-white 1958 Buick stopped and told me to get in and put my bag in the back seat. I was glad to have a ride, so I climbed in. He had a nice car by my standards, a Buick Special two-door sedan, clean, in good condition. The driver was about forty, with a full head of dark wavy hair combed back on all sides and on top. He had a meaty face with broken veins on his cheeks, and his eyes were yellowed and bleary with shadowy lower eyelids. He wore a brown blazer, an open-necked white shirt with a gold chain showing, and tan dress pants. He reminded me of Jackie Gleason when Gleason wasn't being funny, which for me was most of the time. This guy did not try to be a comedian. He said he was going to Los Angeles, which was good news to me. He said his name was

Howard and he was from San Rafael. I remembered where the place was, north of San Francisco, across the bay from the route I had just traveled, and near San Quentin. He said he was in business for himself, and he seemed confident. He smoked Lucky Strikes, non-filtered.

South of Salinas, we came into open country again, hilly, with green fields. In one pasture, a group of three horses looked at us across the fence as we passed by.

In Soledad, Howard stopped to fill the tank. He paid for it with a folded wad of bills from his shirt pocket. As he went to pull out on the highway, he stopped and asked me if I would like to drive. I was still happy at the prospect of a long ride, so I said yes.

Out on the highway again, he reached under the seat and brought out a brown paper bag with a pint bottle of whiskey in it. The bottle was not full. He took to drinking from it. He turned on the radio and tuned in to a station that played songs like "I Walk the Line" and "I've Got a Tiger by the Tail." Howard drank his whiskey and sang along.

In King City, he had me pull over so he could buy another bottle. I waited in the car while he went in, and he came out smiling. Back on the road, he went to work on the second bottle, which was a fifth of Jim Beam. He turned up the radio and sang along with "Your Cheatin' Heart" and "North to Alaska." A Jim Reeves song came on, "He'll Have to Go," and between verses as he sang along, Howard told me that this was the first song he heard on the radio when he bought this car.

He drank and sang and talked as I drove along. Darkness fell, but there was light enough inside the car that I could see him take pills from a stash wrapped in aluminum foil and tucked in the glove box, which had a light when he opened it. He began talking about women and how there was nothing better than a good one and nothing worse than a bad one. His voice became more slurred as the miles rolled by, and his sentence did not hold together as well. Once when he turned to look straight at me, his eyes rolled up into his head, and I could see that he was wasted. He was now snorting every five or ten minutes and spitting out the window, and once in a while he would throw out a live cigarette butt.

At one point he turned to me and said, "What did you say our name was?"

"Jim," I said. "Like Jim Reeves."

"Uh-huh." He nodded, and he looked like a wreck to me.

A little while later, after dozing off a couple of times, he said he was going to coast for a while. He shifted in his seat, turned his head to the right, and went to sleep. I could hear him heaving and breathing. I felt good enough to drive that car all the way to LA, so I settled in for a calm, peaceful drive.

Salinas to Paso Robles is about a hundred miles, less than two hours but close to it with the stops we had made. When we were in the hilly country near Paso Robles, the air coming in through the window was getting cold. Howard's head was leaning on the window ledge, so I pulled the car over, got out, and went around to his side. I opened the door and stuck my hand in to hold his head, and Howard almost fell out. As I put my hip and shoulder against him and pushed him back up into the seat, I thought he was pretty limp. I rolled up the window and turned to straighten Howard up a little better, and he still seemed very limp. I felt for a pulse and got nothing. I put my hand close to his nose and mouth, and I felt no breath. After all of his snoring and heavy breathing, that was a big change. I pushed him one way and another, and he did not tense or respond. Even a passed-out drunk will react in some way. I felt his forehead, his cheek, and his neck, and I thought his body temperature was going down. I tried for a pulse again, held my palm close to feel a breath, and accepted the probable conclusion that Howard was dead.

I opened the glove box and saw only a crumpled piece of aluminum foil. I pulled the bottle from the paper bag and saw about two fingers of whiskey in the bottom. I did not know what to do with these things, so I left them as they were. I closed the car door, went around to the driver's side, and slid in. The tank was well over half full, so I decided to drive on and think about it.

As I drove, the light from the dashboard and from oncoming cars kept me aware of Howard being there. His body was slumped in an unnatural position and in what I thought was plain view. My vague idea was to drive for at least this tank of gas and then do something, but I did not like the way his body looked.

I pulled over and got out. I opened the trunk and saw a suitcase. I did not think I could wrestle a dead body up into that space, and I did not want to try right here on the side of the road where a car could come by at any minute. I decided to put him in the back seat, laid out. I closed the trunk, went around to the passenger side, and opened the door.

The body almost fell out, so I grabbed it and eased it to the ground. At that moment, I realized that this was a two-door and not a four-door. Even if it had been a four-door, I don't know if I could have gotten him up into the back seat. But with the two-door, it was impossible. I tried from inside the car and from outside, but the dead weight was too much. It sagged one way and another, rolled and shifted, no matter what I tried. A couple of cars went by, and I was glad nobody stopped.

As I stood by the car catching my breath, I remembered the money in his shirt pocket. I don't know how many times I had thought about what I would do if I found a wallet along the roadway. I had a similar thought now. I took the folded bills from his shirt pocket, counted them for a total of a hundred and twelve dollars, and put them in my own pocket. Under the circumstances, it did not seem like a theft to me.

I still did not know what to do with the body, but I was sure I could not get it up into the car by myself. I knew I could drag something like that downhill, though, and there was a gully that fell away off the right side of the road. Even that was not easy, but once I got started, I had to stay with it. I dragged the body to what seemed like the bottom, though I couldn't tell in the dark, and I stashed it in some thick brush.

As I stood up straight to catch my breath again, it occurred to me to check for his wallet. I found it in his pants pocket, and in the faint moonlight, I saw that it had money. I decided I would leave the wallet with the car, in the glove box. I did not decide whether I would take the money or leave it in the wallet. I did not have a definite idea of how far I would drive the car, but now it seemed as if I could drive it beyond the current tank of gas if I wanted to. As for the money, I thought, what good would it do Howard at this point, anyway?

I heard a big truck roar by on the highway above, and I told myself to quit dallying around. Someone could stop to see if I need help—or worse, a cop could pull over. I hurried back up to the roadside, pulling in deep breaths by the time I got there, and I was relieved to see the Buick sitting by itself, quiet, in the moonlight. I took long enough to compare Howard's name on the wallet with the name on the registration on the sun visor, and it checked. His name was Howard Capps. I put the wallet in the glove box and took off.

For the first while as I drove the car by myself, I had a sense of freedom, rocketing along a dark highway in a high-powered car. I ran for a while at sixty-five, seventy, eighty, ran it up to a hundred, watching the horizontal orange bar on the speedometer shoot to the right, and brought it down to sixty-five. I did not want to get stopped. I liked driving the car at a reasonable, steady speed, but at no point did I feel that it was mine or that I had taken it. I was just using it to get where I was going.

As my thoughts settled down, I realized it would look like a theft if I was caught. I thought back to the moment when I decided not to try any longer to put the body into the car. Up until then, I could have done things in some different way, I didn't know what, but once I decided to leave Howard there, I couldn't go back and redo it or undo it. I was stuck with what I had done.

On one hand, I thought I should get rid of the car as soon as I could, and on the other, I thought I should be able to use it a little longer. I wasn't hurting anyone.

As I cruised at a steady speed, I began to feel the presence of Howard's suitcase in the trunk. I drove through San Luis Obispo, found the bus station, and left the suitcase in the waiting area. After that, I found a trash can for the whiskey bottle and brown bag.

Back on the road, I felt lighter, more relaxed, but before long my eyes began to droop. I was tired. All of the exertion of trying to get Howard into the car and then of dragging him down into the gully and climbing out was starting to catch up on me. I began to doubt whether I could drive all the way to LA. I realized that I had been thinking in terms of LA because that was where Howard had said he was going, and I had it in the back of my mind to leave the Buick somewhere in that big city and go on to San Diego County on my own.

I thought about stopping at a motel. They would take down my license plate number and maybe even ask to see my driver's license, although I had never had that happen. I decided to do what I knew how to do, and that was to pull behind a gas station that was closed and to sleep for a while. That was a good way to have a cop wake me up, but in my experience, they just told someone to move along. So I thought I would fill up the tank and be ready to go if I needed to.

I went through Pismo Beach and Arroyo Grande and stopped at a gas station set back from the road with a big turning area. I stood outside the car and stretched while the attendant filled the tank and washed the windshield.

A voice at my elbow caused me to turn. A woman had

walked up to me, a bleached blonde with dark eyebrows and dark eyes. She was a little older than I was, between twenty-five and thirty. She wore a short jacket, a tight sweater, a tight skirt, and Nancy Sinatra boots.

"I'm waiting for a bus," she said.

I nodded.

"You could help me save my bus fare, and I could help you pay for gas."

I couldn't help looking her over, and I said, "That would be all right."

"Let me get my bag," she said. "My name's Shirley. I've got someone with me."

She walked away, and I paid for the gasoline. By now I had the money from Howard's shirt pocket in my wallet, with my own money in front of it. I used my money to pay.

Shirley came back carrying a small traveling bag. Half a step behind her was a guy about thirty, carrying a smaller bag, the kind that sailors called an AWOL bag.

"This is Doug," she said.

I waited to hear whether he was a husband or boyfriend, but she didn't say any more. He was about thirty years old, medium height and build, with light-colored, dry hair combed back all the way around. He had a prominent Adam's apple, a slender face, and ears that stuck out. For a moment he reminded me of a picture of Porter Wagoner on the cover of an album I did not buy. He wore a collarless lightweight jacket, a sweatshirt, hopsack jeans, and hush puppies.

His voice startled me when he said, "Put the bags in the back seat?" It was deeper than the voice of any singer I had heard talking on television.

"Sure," I said.

He opened the passenger's door, tipped the seat forward, and tossed the two bags in with mine. Shirley said something in a low voice, and he crawled into the back seat. She smoothed her skirt, sat in the front, and closed the door.

I went around to my side and took my place behind the wheel. After a look in the rearview mirror, I pulled out on the road. I figured I had to keep driving now, but I was awake. The hem of Shirley's skirt had crept up a little, and she didn't pull it down. She made pleasant conversation. She asked me what my name was and where I was from.

I gave her my first name and said I was from Chico. My family had moved around so much when I was growing up that I didn't have an actual hometown, but that was the place I always went back to.

Doug's voice took me by surprise when he asked me where Chico was. I told him it was up north of Sacramento, in the Sacramento Valley.

Shirley asked me what kind of work I did, and I told her I did farmwork. She asked me where I was going, and I told her to see my girlfriend, which was always a safe thing to say. She asked me where that was, and I told her it was down by San Diego.

I began to have the feeling that Shirley had a hunch that the Buick wasn't my car. I hoped she didn't look in the glove box and find Howard's wallet. I thought of a story about Howard being a cousin I had left off in the sanatorium in Weimar, which was a place I had heard about, and I knew it was not a good story. I wished I had put the wallet somewhere else.

To break the silence, I said, "Where are you folks headed?"

Doug's voice from the back seat startled me again. "Tucson."

"That's good," I said, although I couldn't have told him why.

I drove on past Santa Maria, which was built up now with all the new work at the Air Force base, and then Buellton, which was dark and quiet. The highway went out along the coast for a while, another dark stretch, and then it went right through Santa Barbara, with hitchhikers lined up even that late at night.

When we came to Ventura, it was after midnight. I was tired again, stretching and yawning, and I didn't know if I wanted to let Doug drive. I figured I would fall asleep in the back seat and wouldn't know what was going on.

Shirley spoke up in a clear voice. "I'll tell you what, Jim. It's late, and there's still a long ways to go. We could get a motel. Nothing fancy, just something to sleep in. If you pay for the room, we'll fill the gas tank in the morning."

There was something friendly in her voice, so I took the old highway through town. I passed a couple of older motels, one with its lights out.

"Let's get something first," she said. "Pull in here."

I saw that she meant a liquor store, so I parked in front of the door. She turned to Doug and said, "We'll be back in a minute."

I took that as a cue to go in with her, which I didn't mind. She picked out a quart of rum and two large bottles of Coke and stood with her elbow touching mine as we waited at the counter.

The young fellow on duty wore a white shirt and a narrow tie and had his hair combed like the Everly Brothers. As he rang up the items, Shirley asked for two packs of Raleighs with filters. He smiled at her as he set them on the counter. She smiled back and asked if he could give us some ice, so he shook out a clear plastic bag and put a couple of scoops of ice in it. She let me pay, and we went out to the car, where Doug had been waiting.

She picked out an inexpensive-looking, old-fashioned motel, the kind with a flat roof, cement block walls, and parking in front of each room. It had a few cypress trees and juniper bushes.

I went in by myself. On the way, I memorized the license

number, NSJ 156, yellow numbers on a black plate. I told the clerk I needed a room for three people, and he offered me a room with a double bed and a sleeping sofa for ten dollars. I told him I would take it. He did not ask for my driver's license, so I registered in Howard's name and wrote down the license number of the Buick. I took the room key with me, parked the car in front of Room 12 and said, "Here we are."

Inside, under a bright light, Shirley mixed drinks of rum and Coke and ice. She took off her boots and sat on the couch, while Doug and I each sat on a chair. They lit cigarettes, and I sipped on my rum and Coke, which I was not used to.

The first drink went down, and as Shirley was getting ready to mix some more, she said, "Doug, why don't you go out and find us some sandwiches or hamburgers?"

He gave a sour look and said, in his deep voice, "Where in the hell am I goin' to find somethin' to eat at this hour?"

"There's always someplace open in a town this size. I'm hungry, and I'm sure Jim is, too. Aren't you?"

I was feeling tipsy, and I thought I could use something to eat. "I guess I am," I said.

"See? Look Doug. If you go, I bet Jim will give you the money. What do you think, Jim? It won't be more than five dollars."

"I guess I could." I took out my wallet, and the smallest bill in front was a ten. I gave it to her, and she gave it to Doug.

He did not seem to be in a good mood, but he stood up. His deep voice came out in a grouchy tone. "Am I supposed to walk?"

Shirley turned to me and said, "You don't mind if he takes your car, do you?"

"Oh, no," I said. I fished into my pocket for the keys and gave them to him.

When I heard the car start up and back away, I remembered Howard's wallet, and I hoped like hell that Doug didn't look in the glove box.

Shirley finished mixing the drinks on the low table and said, "Why don't you come sit next to me?"

I couldn't have said no even if I had had nothing to drink. I sat on the couch next to her, took the drink she handed me, and tried to stay calm.

"You don't talk much," she said. "Are you the quiet type, or are you just shy to begin with?"

"I don't know."

"I think there's more to you than meets the eye. Are you just thinking of your girlfriend?"

"She's not all that much of a girlfriend. I just went out with her once."

"Then you're not...going steady. I wondered." She put her hand on my leg. "But I know you like girls. I don't wonder about that."

Things swirled in a way that seemed to be a rush of silence, and our lips met in a kiss. It was the kind of kiss I had known before, wet with a taste of cigarette smoke and alcohol and no holding back. In another minute, we were together on the couch, and in a minute or two more, we were done, breathing hard.

"We'd better get straightened up before Doug comes back," she said. "That was good, though."

We drew apart and got our clothes back in order. I took my drink and sat in my chair again. She lit a cigarette and sat close to the table to smoke it between sips on her drink.

She had finished her cigarette when Doug came back. He had three lunch-meat-and-cheese sandwiches wrapped in cellophane, and he gave me seven dollars in change.

He wrinkled his nose and glared at Shirley, and his voice boomed. "What did you do when I was gone?"

"Nothing," she said. "Sit down and eat your sandwich. I'll fix you a drink."

"I think you did something. What in the hell did you do?"

"Nothing, I tell you." She stared at him with her dark eyes. "What did you do?"

"I went and found these sandwiches."

"Good. Let's eat. It's late."

"I want to know what you did." His voice seemed to fill the room.

"Jesus," she said. "Leave it alone."

"You take me for a dummy."

"I take you for one if you don't leave it alone and forget about it."

Doug turned his eyes on me. They were light brown, with puffy lower eyelids. "I ought to knock your block off."

"Leave him alone," Shirley said. "He didn't do anything."

"Send me out for sandwiches. How stupid do you think I am?"

"Don't get a bug in your ass. No one did anything." She poured him a drink and reached toward me. "Finish that, and I'll make you another one."

I had drunk almost all of my second drink in a few minutes, out of nervousness, and it was starting to catch up with me. I rattled the ice against my teeth as I finished it, and I handed her my glass.

Doug's voice made me flinch. "Son of a bitch. Did you make it strong enough?" He frowned at his glass.

"It's good for what ails you."

She mixed my drink and handed it to me, and I could tell she had put plenty of rum in it as well. But the Coke made it go down smooth. I unwrapped my sandwich and ate it. The others did the same, and I was not aware of much else going on in the room. My head was swimming, and I think I finished my third drink.

———

I AWOKE with a throbbing headache as full daylight streamed through the thin curtains. I had a terrible dry taste in my mouth and throat, and my stomach felt as if it was going to revolt. I was lying on my side on the floor, with my head tipped crooked. I had no pillow and no blanket, and I had such a feeling of dread that I did not want to move.

My first thought was that they took the car. I pushed myself up onto one elbow and saw Shirley stretched out on the couch. She was still dressed, and her legs were crossed.

I sat up, and my head pounded. My traveling bag was on the floor next to me, and my wallet was next to it. I reached for my wallet and opened it. All the money was gone.

I pushed down the sick feeling in my throat, stood up, and took a few unsteady steps until I could lean against the window trim and peek out past the edge of the curtain. The Buick was gone. I was not surprised. But Shirley was still here.

I pushed away from the window and turned toward the couch where she was sprawled on her back with her eyes closed and her mouth open. I blinked and focused, and a strange feeling rose inside me as I saw bruise marks on her throat.

I touched her, and she did not move. She was not loose like Howard. She was beginning to stiffen.

A tingling surge of fear ran all through me, from my arms and legs up to my face and scalp. My eyes swelled. My face was hot and throbbing with my pulse. I had such a thick feeling in my throat that I couldn't swallow.

I went to the bathroom, splashed my face with cold water, and drank out of my hand. I thought I was going to throw up, but my stomach was nauseous and empty with only the aftertaste of rum and Coke rising to my throat.

I had a strange, detached feeling as I took soft steps back to the couch. Shirley had not moved and was not going to. I felt her face, and it did not have body warmth.

I could only imagine what had happened after I passed out. Doug had not let things go. He had taken his anger out on Shirley, and he had left me to take the rap. He would be hours away from here by now. If he was really on his way to Tucson, he could be driving on the freeway east of LA, headed to San Bernardino and beyond. Or he could have left the car in LA as I had thought to do and was sitting in a bus.

For a moment I gazed at Shirley, the life gone out of her. It didn't make any sense. Maybe she had played me along with her friendly conversation and then her kootchie-koo, but I thought the last part was one of those wham-bam things that people do when they have a chance. I thought the two of them might have had some idea of taking the car or at least of getting as much out of me as they could, but in the end, they weren't the same kind of person. They did not have that code of honor among thieves or whatever it was that held people together when they were out to get the best of someone else.

But I knew one thing. I was not going to take the rap for this if I could help it. If I stayed around, everything about Howard would come out as well. I made myself concentrate. The hotel clerk did not have my name. My fingerprints were all over the place, but they weren't on file anywhere in this part of the state. I needed to get out of Ventura as soon as I could without attracting any attention. Checkout time was at noon, so I had about an hour and a half. I needed to walk out of there calm and slow, make my way to the edge of town, and catch a ride.

———

ALL THAT DAY, I felt poisoned from the rum and the syrup in the Coke and whatever chemicals had been let loose inside my body from the shock and the surge of fear. Complete dread ran through me. My nerves were jangled. When I got a ride and spoke to the driver, my voice sounded as if it came from outside of me. I was dazed and dry-mouthed and empty, not just hungry, but hollow down to my feet. The day itself was dry and bright, then glaring as my rides took me down along the west side of Lost Angeles through the smog. It seemed like a different time of year and a different world from the one I had left the day before, and time dragged on with long waits between rides.

Night fell before I was out of the LA area. I saw signs for Long Beach, Huntington Beach, Irvine. At last, a ride left me off in Oceanside. Fog had rolled in, and the night was dark, as I trudged along the highway toward Vista. All day in the glare of LA and in the company of other people, I had not thought much about what I was going to do when I got to this point. Now I felt as if something bad was going to happen to me.

I think the shock of finding Shirley was starting to wear off, along with the bleariness of the rum and Coke. I was a long way from Ventura, and I did not think anyone would be looking for me on foot. They would be looking for the car and a man named Howard Capps. But I still had a sense of fate hanging over me. I realized again that from the moment I left Howard where I did, it could be considered that I stole the money and the car, even though I did not have either of them now. I had also failed to report his death and Shirley's, and they were tied up together through me. I felt jumpy about every aspect of where I was and what could happen to me. I had no idea of what I would tell Linda. She wasn't even expecting me. I hadn't thought to call her again until I was out of money.

I stopped on the side of the road in the dark and fog, and I decided I would be just as well off if I went back to where I came from. I walked across the highway and began walking to Oceanside.

———

IT MUST HAVE BEEN the early morning hours when I found the on-ramp going north. I had walked off my nervousness, but I was dull-minded and tired and hungry. I sat down with my back against the freeway entrance sign and fell asleep. Twice I woke up as cars went past me. When the sky began to lighten in the east, I stood up and put out my thumb. Daylight was spreading across the freeway when I got a ride to San Clemente.

For the rest of the morning, I had short rides and intervals of waiting. I went where my rides took me, and I ended up on the coast highway. A man in a Mustang who told me he carried a .38 bought me lunch and left me off at an intersection on the north side of Long Beach. I walked past it to a wide spot where cars could stop.

I felt that I needed to get over to the other side of LA and find the highway to Bakersfield. I had seen on a map that it was a freeway now, but people still called it Highway 99. I thought that if I was lucky, I could make it to the Grapevine by night.

My eyes were tired, and I squinted in the sun. A crew doing roadwork was putting out a lot of dust and noise. Each time the light changed, cars came at me from the intersection. I was surprised when a pale-green 1964 Chrysler pulled over. A clean-cut man in a jacket and tie was driving, and in the back seat, a dark-haired man in a brown embroidered jacket and a cream-colored shirt with pearl snaps put on a brown hat as he let down the window. He had a guitar on the seat next to him, and he reminded me of Johnny Horton.

In a smooth voice, he said, "We're goin' up the coast highway, through Malibu, then onto 101 to Santa Maria. You're welcome to ride in front."

I winced. "I'm trying to get over to 99 so I can go up north through Bakersfield."

"You can ride with us up to Ventura, take Highway 126 across through Santa Paula, Fillmore, and Piru, and catch the freeway at Castaic Junction. It'll take you over the Grapevine and on into Bakersfield. We travel it from time to time, and there's nothin' to it, but you can judge for yourself."

I didn't like the idea of being on foot near Ventura, but it sounded like a good way to get out of LA. I thought I could decide when I reached Ventura whether I wanted to get out or ride with them a little farther north. So I accepted the ride and settled into the front seat with my bag at my feet.

The upholstery was soft, off-white leather, very nice, and the Chrysler had a smooth, quiet motor. I drowsed off as we went through the towns on the coast, and I was awake when we went through Santa Monica and on to Pacific Palisades. The day was clear with a sunny blue sky and a beautiful view out over the ocean. Past Malibu, the man in the back seat began strumming his guitar. He said he had a show that night in Santa Maria. He said he was from Eastern Colorado and he made a living playing for homesick Okies up and down the line from LA to Sacramento.

I understood him to mean all those people who came out from Oklahoma, Texas, Arkansas, and other places during the Depression. I knew them in school and worked with them in the fields. I said, "Do you know Okie Paul Westmoreland?"

"Yes, I do," he said. "I know Ola Louise, too. They're in Sacramento now."

I said, "I heard him on the radio when I was a little kid, up by Chico and Paradise."

He strummed a little more and sang two lines.

I know that you came all the way from Texas
To see if I would give you one more chance.

He started over and sang again, with a different second line.

I know that you came all the way from Texas

To see if I would take you back again.

He played those two versions back and forth a few times, and I wished he would do the whole song, but he quit singing when the driver slowed down.

We had left sight of the ocean for a little while and were alongside it again. The car ahead of us was just plugging along. My pulse went up when I saw that it was a blue-and-white Buick.

The chauffeur stepped on it to go around, and I turned to see what kind of a person was driving the car. I half expected to see Doug with his fluffy hair, jug ears, and prominent Adam's apple, but I saw a dumpy, middle-aged guy with dark hair slicked back like Elvis Presley. He was singing with the radio. The window was open, but I couldn't tell what song it was. The chauffeur kept accelerating, and we went around.

Now the guy in the Buick decided to speed up. He pulled out, passed us, and slowed down again. I didn't know what to think, but I looked at the license plate and saw that it wasn't the NSJ 156, even though the car looked just like the one I had driven.

The chauffeur passed him again, and the Buick sped up and stayed right behind the Chrysler.

The chauffeur looked in his rearview mirror and said, "I don't know why he's got to be right on my ass."

The man in the back seat said, "Don't let 'em pull any shit, Tommy."

"I won't."

The Buick passed us again, rocking side to side, and Tommy slowed down. He said, "I'll let him get way ahead."

He found a wide spot on the other side of the road and parked the Chrysler with its nose pointing out toward the ocean. He and the boss got out and stood looking at the rippling waves, so I did, too. I thought we were an unlikely trio—the singer in his hat and embroidered jacket and polished boots, the driver in his gray suit with a shoulder holster that was showing as he had unbuttoned his jacket, and me in my worn and wrinkled traveling clothes. We took in the calm afternoon for a few minutes and got back into the car.

When we were under way, Tommy said, "I don't know what that guy thought he was up to, but I like to have people like that in front of me."

I settled into my ride again. I thought about the anxious time I would have on the highway that the singer mentioned. I asked Tommy where he thought he would leave me off.

He said, "Highway 126 comes in on this side of Ventura, so I won't leave you off in town unless you want me to."

I said, "No, that'll be all right. Where the highway comes in." I was worried, but I hoped I wouldn't spend much time there and could make it to the Grapevine by night.

The sun had crossed into late afternoon when Tommy pulled over and let me out. I thanked both of them and began walking along the highway. Up ahead, I saw a sign for Santa Paula and Fillmore. I had not reached the sign when a Volkswagen stopped for me.

My second ride took me through orange and lemon country, where I saw workers coming out of a lemon orchard with their empty picking bags. I wondered if I would ever end up working down this way. My third ride took me to the new freeway, where a young fellow in a white van was finishing his day of delivering delicatessen products. He took me north through Gorman, Lebec, and Mettler and left me off at a truck stop in Bakersfield.

A truck driver picked me up and said he was going to Sacramento. I breathed a big sigh when I put Bakersfield behind me. The driver had a new eight-track tape player, and for my entertainment, I think, he put in a tape of truck-driving songs. I had heard most of them before, but I perked up in that part of "Six Days on the Road" when the guy says he's takin' little white pills and his eyes are open wide. I wondered what kind of pills Howard had taken. When the tape was over, I fell asleep. I woke up a couple of times in places like Merced and Manteca, although Madera and Modesto were in there as well. It was a jumbled sleep in a noisy cab, but it took me to a truck stop on the north side of Sacramento, where the damp, chilly air seemed like home to me.

BACK IN CHICO, I tried to settle into a normal life again. I went to the employment office and found work pruning trees and piling brush. It was cold work, wet half the time, but it paid $1.75 an hour. I stayed in a cabin court and rode back and forth with another guy. But I always felt that I was looking over my shoulder.

I kept thinking about what a poor idea it was not to try to do something else with Howard. Everything went back to that moment. If I had done something different, I wouldn't have ended up with Doug and Shirley. And even if I had found myself in a situation like that, I could have stuck it out if I hadn't had my earlier mistake hanging over me.

I couldn't get over seeing Shirley dead on the couch where I had had the quickie with her, and I wondered what it took for Doug to do something like that. I also remembered telling them where I was from. I thought that if the law caught up with Doug, he could tell them where to look for me. He would try to put the blame on me. He might even have my last name. He had opened my wallet to take all the money.

Time went on like that for a couple of weeks. Thanksgiving passed, and it was close to the end of the month. It was always dark by the time I got home from work, and I went out and did my errands after I ate. One evening as I was leaving my room on my way to buy some lunch meat and cheese, a two-toned car of red-orange and white, a '55 or '56 Ford, stopped up ahead of me. A man in a short-brimmed hat got out and walked around the front of the car, looking down. As I passed the front fender, he straightened up and showed me a flat gun, shining dark in the glow of the streetlight. His deep voice sent a jolt all the way through me.

"Get in the car. You're goin' to drive."

Doug. After everything I had been through—getting out of Ventura, going all the way to Oceanside for no purpose, making my way around Ventura again, coming back north some four or five hundred miles, depending on how you counted it, and settling into a simple life again—here he was. He must have been in town for a while, living off Howard's money and mine. Chico was not that big of a town, and all he had to do was keep an eye on the kinds of places where a guy like me would stay.

He held the gun on me as I got in on the passenger's side and slid across to the steering wheel. He climbed in and told me what to do. I started the car, made a couple of left turns, and drove south out of town. We were on a smaller highway that led to Durham and then Biggs. I knew the road because I had been out that way knocking and raking almonds the year before.

Doug asked me how I liked driving this car, and I didn't answer.

A few miles out, he told me to slow down and park. I pulled off on the side by an almond orchard, all bare branches in the moonlight when I shut off the engine and lights.

He had me lock the driver's door and scoot out of the car the way I had gone in. He took the keys and locked the passenger's door, then had me walk on a diagonal through the orchard. I wondered if he was going to shoot me and leave me there, until we came to an open area where a large corrugated metal building cast a shadow. He prodded me around to a door that opened, and once we were inside, he turned on a flashlight.

I could see that it was the kind of a big shed where someone would hull almonds and separate the rocks and dirt clods. I saw frames and horizontal screens and conveyor belts and elevators with sprockets and chains. Metal stairs and a catwalk led to a big hopper, which would feed the almonds onto the screens to be shaken and then passed on to the next step.

"Over here," he said, in that voice that I never liked.

He backed me up against a metal stairway, tucked the flashlight under the arm of his gun hand, and took out a wallet. It looked like Howard's.

He kept his voice low as he said, "Put this in your pocket."

I took it and put it in the pocket of my work shirt. I thought I saw what he meant to do, which was to force me up the stairs and push me off into the hopper or onto the metal equipment below. From his quiet movements and his low voice, I had a hunch that he didn't want to fire the gun and make a noise. I didn't want to call his bluff, though, and get a bullet for my trouble.

He took the flashlight in his left hand again, and I realized that he had both hands full. I took that instant to grab his right wrist with both my hands and to move out of the line of fire. He tried to hit me with the flashlight, but I jerked him. He pulled back, and for a moment we were both yanking and lurching until I bent his arm and pushed on him. The gun went off, the flashlight fell to the floor, and Doug let out a strange sound like *ugh-gh* as he took in a breath. He slumped to the floor, and the gun rattled on the concrete.

I picked up the flashlight and held it on him. Blood was seeping out of the corner of his mouth, and his eyes were blank. His upper teeth pressed on his lower lip, and I thought he was going to make the *F* sound, but a horrid expression came to his face, and I turned the light away.

I straightened up and stood back. I had to think fast. I had seen a house not far away before we went into the metal building. I needed to get out of there, but I had to think of details. I needed the keys. I did not want to touch the gun. I should put the wallet in Doug's pocket and leave the flashlight. Then I needed to get out and stay in the dark.

My heart was pounding as I moved through the orchard on a fast walk, clutching the car keys. Thoughts raced through my head. I could drive to town, grab my things, and move on to some other place. But I would have to ditch the car, and someone could track me. I would be looking over my shoulder for the rest of my life. My fingerprints might be on the gun. I didn't think so, but they would be on the wallet and the flashlight. At some point the hotel clerk could identify me, and I could take the rap for Shirley. Howard's car would turn up, and someone, someday, would find Howard.

I stopped for a minute to catch my breath and let my thoughts settle. In that dark orchard with the bare branches above me, I admitted to myself that in spite of what I thought my intentions had been, I stole Howard's car and money. That was what it became when I hid his body. And I ran from my responsibility in Ventura because I was afraid of everything together. Now I owed it to Shirley to bring Doug to account even if he was dead.

I took a deep breath and recognized what I should do—face up to the wrong things I did, accept my part of the blame, and set the record straight about what happened to Shirley. On the other hand, as I imagined going back to that same police station, I thought I would be a fool to turn myself in and run the risk of getting stuck with all the blame after all. I knew that that was sometimes the way they did things.

I made my way to the edge of the orchard, found the car, and tried to see if I could tell the door key from the ignition key. The two keys looked the same, not a round one and a square one. As I tried the first key, lights appeared on the road from town—bright headlights and a flashing red light.

I fumbled the keys and dropped them. I knelt to look for them in the shadows cast by the headlights. The patrol car slowed and stopped. I found the keys and stood up. My heart was beating in my throat as a cop in a cap and jacket came around in front of the headlights.

"I'd like to talk to you for a minute," he said. "Put your hands on the roof of the car."

When he had patted me down, he told me to turn around.

"What is it?" I said.

"We had a report of a gunshot, and I'd like to know what you're doing here."

I didn't have a story. "I don't know," I said.

"Let's go sit in the unit, then." He walked me to the patrol car, opened the back door and said, "Put your hands in back of you." He put the handcuffs on me, and I got in.

He closed the door, went around to the driver's side, and got in. He looked at me through the screen and said, "We'll try it again. What do you know?"

I pictured Doug lying on the floor not very far from there, and I thought, this was it. "Quite a bit," I said. "I just don't want to take the blame for something I didn't do. I'll tell the truth and take my chances."

The River

A Rowdy Story

Chris Mullen

The River

"DIS BE A BAD TING."

Mac's words. A warning. His deep voice, so foreign, so mysterious, and even when he whispered, powerful. His words cycled through my mind as if caught in the swirl of a gully washer's muddy tirade after a torrential downpour. I sat at the bow of the riverboat *Delilah* and watched the water lap up against the front of the boat.

"River pirates," I whispered to myself.

It was midmorning. With Captain Jim Hennessy at the helm, and Mac working his push pole in and out of the water, we headed south on the Mississippi River. We had been riding with the southerly currents for what felt like hours on end, though it had only been a short time since we set off from the docks in St. Louis, Missouri. Bathed in sunlight, my mind was adrift in the chaos of what I had witnessed two nights ago.

Men in skiffs, silent killers waiting for the right moment, and then...

I closed my eyes and tried to think of anything else, but the shadowy figures that charged ashore with arms raised and weapons poised for attack, haunted me. Their violent, bloodthirsty yells mixed with the victims terrified screams and agonizing groans. The sound echoed in my head like the ongoing gong of a church bell. The lingering vibrations were so crisp, so real, it caused the hairs on my neck to stand and flooded my body with an icy sensation of dread. I pressed my palms to my ears but was unable to shake the memory.

"Hey. You okay there, son?"

I jumped at the feel of a powerful hand on my shoulder and looked up to see Captain Hennessy. His tall, wide figure blocked the sun, appearing to look more like a massive shadow that loomed over me than a man.

"Keep a watchful eye, now. Lots ta see out'n the river. The currents 'er always playin' games with us. Changin' where they're at. Tryin' to run us aground. So far, yer doin' fine. Just remember ta keep yer eyes ahead as we go."

"Yessir," I said. "I was just thinkin' back to the other night."

"Don't you worry, son. Ain't nothin' like that gonna happen ta us."

Hennessy gave me a firm nod, his lips curled and pressed up just under his nose. He was reassuring, but I had my doubts.

It was half past nine. Sunlight gleamed on the rippling water like campfire sparks shooting into the night sky. A slight headwind brushed my face and caused my hair to flip back and forth between gusts. I kept my eyes ahead as instructed but felt that there was little chance of escaping an attack on the water without a fight. The danger on the river was real.

Delilah was a keelboat and was stocked full of goods—boxes of fabrics and cloth, bales of cotton wrapped in burlap, tobacco packed in hogshead barrels, small casks of gunpowder, and stacks of wooden crates with various items—all destined for New Orleans, Louisiana.

The current pulled us along, and Mac steered as we went, but when Captain Hennessy called me over, I learned what lay hidden under the tarp on the starboard side of *Delilah*. He called it his "secret weapon." I thought it was a cannon or some kind of weapon to help protect us. I could not have been more wrong.

"This here contraption gets us where we're goin' faster'n most," Captain Hennessy said, pulling the tarp aside.

Hidden beneath the tarp was a small-scale version of a paddle wheel like ones I had seen on bigger riverboats that carried travelers and gamblers to different cities along the Mississippi. Captain Hennessy had devised a way to install a small water-tube boiler that generated enough steam to power the blades of the paddle wheel at various speeds. While fuel for the boiler took up its fair share of space onboard, the benefit of being able to churn against the river current gave us a huge advantage over other cargo ships. He explained that we could deliver goods quicker than most of our competitors.

"The faster we deliver, the more jinglin' in our pockets. Ya got me?" Captain Hennessy said, patting the front pockets of his trousers.

While he said his design was a secret, it was obvious to me that once it was uncovered and engaged, the paddle wheel contraption would be in plain sight. I asked what would stop others from copying his design.

"People kin look all they want, 'cept they cain't get a glimpse of what's in here," he said, tapping a finger on the side of his head. "That's where the real secret lies."

I learned right then that while Captain Hennessy may have the appearance of a run-of-the-mill riverboat captain, his mind was classes above the rest.

As the day progressed, I was able to cast aside the visions of the river pirates, but thoughts of my father and brother's murder swept in to fill the void. Had it not been for the raid at my home, I would never have been put in the position I was in now—barely a young man, alone except for the company of Captain Hennessy and Mac, and unsure about what tomorrow would have in store.

"A man acts like one because he has to. A boy acts like one when he wants to. What are you?"

These were the words my father would say to both me and my brother when challenges faced us or problems came between us. They were important and held deep meaning. As I thought about the things he said, the things he taught me, and the time he set aside for my brother and me, I began to feel regret. They were both gone. Forever. It was time I would never get back. My father's wisdom was all I had left of him. Looking out across the water, a pair of cardinals swooped overhead, and I vowed to never forget the lessons he had taught me.

Holding my head high, I resumed my duties as spotter at the bow of *Delilah* and kept a watchful eye as we made our way south along the Big Muddy.

———

THE MISSISSIPPI WAS KIND, but the weather grew hot the farther downriver we traveled. Summer was at hand, and I learned quickly that the South had varying degrees of temperature, most of which resulted in what seemed like barrels of sweat drenching my entire body. Adding to the heat was a despicable feeling, like a thin coat of spilled syrup or honey on my skin. It got all over everything. Every part of my body was affected. From between my fingers to the bend behind my knees—and even those places you are not supposed to mention—felt sticky.

As much as it bothered me, I learned firsthand what would happen when Mac had heard enough of my complaints. When we communicated, which was not often, it was more by action than with words. This time, his message was in the form of me being lifted off the deck and thrown over the rail and into the river. The current was slow, and I was never in any danger, but I scrambled for *Delilah* as if something was after me under the water. When I pulled myself back onboard, Captain Hennessy gave me a look that seemed to say, "It was only a matter of time." Mac was back at his post working his push pole. He may not have been smiling on the outside, but I saw a glimmer in his eye that suggested he had enjoyed throwing me overboard. Truth be told, I am glad he did. I was soaked, but I was much cooler and less sticky than before.

The landscape of the Mississippi River changed as well. The long stretches of open water to which I had become accustomed began to bend and curve like a snake slithering across the ground. This serpentine pattern made it difficult to see around each bend, which kept me on my toes. As the spotter, I had warned Captain Hennessy many times during the voyage about sandbars and large debris to avoid, and I was not going to let this stretch of river get the better of me.

We meandered south along the boundary of Arkansas and the state of Mississippi, which made me wonder if that was where the river got its name.

"Nope, that ain't it," Captain Hennessy said. "Ya see, the river spans more than two thousand miles from New Orleans and the Gulf of Mexico to the headwaters somwhere's up in Minnesota. The name Mississippi is just the way we say it nowadays, but back before even my time, it weren't. French traders peddlin' pelts an' furs an' such got ta know some of the natives. One of the groups was the Ojibwe. They live way up north. They called it *Misi-ziibi*. It means Great Water er Big River. No...Great River, somethin' like that. Anyhows, later when more English-speaking settlers came around, they took ta callin' it Mississippi. That's how the river got its name. State too, if memory serves me, but that's another history lesson, an' I'm only good fer one a day."

Captain Hennessy smiled at me, and for a moment I felt something I had not experienced since before I lost my family. It was not love or affection, but a belonging.

————

THROUGHOUT MY FIRST voyage aboard *Delilah*, I found myself becoming fascinated by new sights and sounds. Most of the sounds were caused by wildlife I saw along the banks and in the trees, while others broke the flow of nature's call. At times I could hear distant voices singing or people on the shore talking. On the water, the thrum and splash of a paddleboat and the music that spilled out of the floating saloons or from musicians playing on deck were pleasant to listen to, but it would only last as long as it took them to pass us by. Smiling, I would pretend to be one of the rich patrons onboard, sunning myself while listening to the delightful music. It was a good image, but only a dream.

I found solace in the soft cooing doves, the harsh call of a blackbird, the melodic and often cheery songs of the summer yellowbird; they all added to the ambiance found only in the choral tapestry of the riverscape.

I was no stranger to the sight of turtles perched atop fallen logs or rocks that poked far enough out of the water to accommodate a bale of the ancient-looking creatures. I loved how they stretched their necks as if they sought to nibble the sunlight, then plopped into the water at the first sign of trouble. What I had not seen before, but had been warned about by Captain Hennessy, were the rigid backs, elongated bodies, and menacing mouths of alligators. He assured me that they preferred quiet bogs and swampy marshes, but that the closer we came to New Orleans, the better chances I would have to see one.

"Just watch yer toes," he joked. "They might look like an easy meal danglin' over the bow like that."

He laughed when I quickly recoiled my feet to sit cross-legged at the bow instead of cooling them in the water as we floated south.

The short time before evening, just as dusk settled in, was the most satisfying for me. The wind felt gentle. Fireflies littered the shoreline, bobbing in the air like lighted tufts of dandelions blowing in the breeze. The lull of the cicada's buzz, and the chirps of crickets and katydids filled the air with soft echoes. The river felt most alive as night swept over the sky. If I timed it just right, I could look straight above me and see the final blend of bright yellows and oranges as they met the first hues of nightfall. The murky blues and rich purples joined the day's last call of color, and like a wave crashing to shore, ushered darkness in to cover everything.

But it would not last. As soon as blackness enveloped us all, a new light began to show itself. The heaven's daily cue revealed another mystery that I failed to understand, but that did not stop me from marveling in its beauty. Patterns and clusters of stars speckled the sky. To me, I envisioned someone sprinkling sugar over us, making the sight that much sweeter.

It was hard for me to pick a favorite time of day. Both were captivating. I also knew that both had hidden dangers.

———

SIX DAYS after loading *Delilah* with our cargo, I stood on the docks in Bayou Belle, Louisiana, a small riverfront town just north of New Orleans. Known for its expansive sugarcane farming and bustling river activity, the trading post and easy portage was what made this a desirable stop for Captain Hennessy.

As we approached the dock, Captain Hennessy positioned *Delilah* at a shallow angle which was ideal for safe docking and allowed for easier adjustments and less impact if something went wrong.

"Geet de bow line reh-dee," Mac called to me.

I grabbed the rope and waited, all the while keeping my eyes on him.

"Dare," he said, pointing as he spoke. "Toss dem to dee man wit dee red hair."

I looked and saw a man waiting for me to catch the bow line. He was not hard to miss. The man had red hair, as Mac had said, but he also had an orange beard growing from his chin that hung to the middle of his chest. He wore tattered overalls and boots but did not have a shirt underneath. His fair skin was red with sunburn. He raised his hands, offering me a target.

"C'mon, boy. Let's see whatcha got."

The rope was heavy. With a heave, I slung it to the red-haired man. He snagged the twisting rope out of the air like it was nothing, then set to work looping it around a dock post. I looked at Mac and saw him toss the stern line to a different dock worker. He then glanced at me and gave a gruff nod of his head that I took as his approval. He went about double-checking the cargo and made sure the ties were secure. Captain Hennessy called me over.

"Come with me. We're gonna see if'n we can't pawn off some of this cargo right here."

"What about Mac?" I asked.

"He's got things ta do. We ain't gonna be here but a short while," he said, pointing to the southern horizon. "Seems like there's a bit a weather blowin' 'round."

I hopped off *Delilah*. My knees buckled beneath me. I had been on the water more than off of it for close to a week, and I was not used to the feel of solid ground. Captain Hennessy smirked and caught me by the back of my shirt to keep me from falling.

"Gotta turn in yer sea legs fer yer land legs, son. Keep up, otherwise yer liable ta get swept off with another'n of these boats. Not ever-one is as they seem in these parts."

"Think some of them could be river pirates?" I asked.

"A-yuh. Wouldn't be surprised a'tall."

I swiveled my head from side to side as we walked. Workers on the docks shouted to one another as they loaded and unloaded crates from other vessels similar to *Delilah*. The air was thick with the scent of fresh produce, fish, and the ever-present muddy aroma of the Mississippi. I took in the sights and sounds, making sure to remember the men that looked, to me, like trouble.

Beyond the docks was a dirt road filled with activity. Children ran around, their laughter blending with the chatter of their mothers who were busy haggling for the best produce. Old men sat in the shade, telling tales that were a mix of river folklore and actual history. From what little I heard made it hard to tell where one ended and the other began.

One man caught my eye, then called out to me.

"Heh, boy. Don't git too close ta Belle Manor." His voice was raspy and his accent was strange, sounding more French in origin but with a drawl as he hung on to some of the words longer than normal. "Dem hauntin' tings goin' on behin' dem windahs."

I stopped and glanced at a large, two-story house on a hill that overlooked the river. It had four large columns in front, giving it the look of an old plantation. A porch ran the length of the white-washed face of the house, and there were more windows than I had ever seen before.

"Dats dee one, boy."

My eyes grew large when I spied movement in the

shadows near Belle Manor, and I shrieked when I felt a large hand on my shoulder.

"Whoa, settle down now. You'll draw attention ta yerself hollerin' like that." Captain Hennessy spoke in a firm voice. "Keep up er head back. Just don't go gettin' lost."

As we walked away, the old man held his gaze on me. He smiled showing the jagged remnants of blackened teeth left to rot in his mouth. Turning my back to him I could still feel his eyes staring me down. It made my flesh crawl.

A hundred yards from the docks was a building with a large sign posted out front. *Trader LeMaire's*. I followed Captain Hennessy inside and was amazed to see so many things—ropes and tarps, clothing, shoes, long rifles, ammunition, dried foods, barrels of tobacco like the ones we hauled, knives, iron hardware and tools, fishing gear, animal traps, furs and pelts—the supplies seemed endless. Captain Hennessy hailed the store proprietor as if they were old friends.

"LeMaire, ya ol' coot."

A man behind the counter looked up and squinted his eyes at Captain Hennessy. He stepped away from what he was doing and walked straight over to him, stopping just when I thought they would collide. *"Que veux-tu, vieux?"*

"Old man?" Captain Hennessy said, placing his hands on his hips, "Who ya callin' old man?"

LeMaire did not reply. His lips curled into a snarl. I could see his fingers clench. I began to grow nervous, thinking, *should I run for Mac?* With one quick motion, LeMaire raised his arms and wrapped Captain Hennessy in a bear hug, lifting him off his feet.

"I think eet ees you I call old man, *ami*. Eet has been a long time, no?"

"Sassafras on Christmas day, put me down," Captain Hennessy demanded.

LeMaire let go and stepped back. "Good to see you."

"You as well," Captain Hennessy said. "Got a load outside I want ya ta have a look at."

LeMaire stroked the stubble on his chin, then saw me watching their exchange. "Who ees thees?" he said, pointing to me.

Captain Hennessy gave me a glance. "New deckhand. Plucked 'im outta the water aways upriver. He may look scrawny, but he took ta workin' like a man, so's I'm keepin' him on as long as he likes."

A warm sense of pride washed over me. Did Captain Hennessy mean what he said? I straightened my stance and stood a little taller.

Looking at me, LeMaire said, "Zees man works you to zee bone, boy?"

"Yessir. I mean, no sir. I do my job just as he said."

The two men laughed.

"Anyone who can stand to work for zees man ees fine by me." LeMaire reached over the counter and pulled out a box filled with green and brown sticks that looked like bamboo.

"Bayou Belle ees famous for eets sugarcane. Take one, boy."

I looked to Captain Hennessy. He nodded, and I reached into the box to pull out one of the cut husks.

"Eet ees so sweet. Better than any candee you weell ever taste."

"Thank you," I said.

Captain Hennessy motioned to the door, but LeMaire paused. "Come an' take a gander at what I'm haulin'. Maybe ya find somethin' that suits ya."

"I weell look, but as you can see, I am almost stocked to zee rafters."

BANG!

I jumped at the sound of gunfire erupting outside, nearly dropping my sugarcane. Captain Hennessy and LeMaire ducked as if they were dodging bullets, then scrambled to the window for a look. I followed close behind.

Tucked behind the two men, I could not see anything. People rushed inside to get out of the line of fire as the blasts continued.

In all the commotion, it was also hard to hear. The chatter rose to a raucous roar as the trading post filled. I saw a boy and his mother rush inside and crouch near the floor.

I tugged Captain Hennessy's arm. "Captain Hen…"

"Shush!" His shortness stung.

The two men turned away from the window and slid down to sit on the floor.

"Ya remember how you was askin' 'bout river pirates? Well, the men doin all the shootin' are doin' a roundup. Happens from time ta time, 'cept they ain't with the law. They see and do things their own way. Some 'round these parts like 'em. To others, they're just as bad if not worse than the river pirates themselves."

"Zey call themselves zee Swampside Gang," LeMaire added. "Zey are no friends of mine. *Que ces enfoirés pourrissent en enfer!*"

I had no idea what the last thing he said meant, but by the sounds of it, it was not good.

The gunfire stopped, but a new-sounding boom added to the building tension outside. The window grew dark, and the wind began to blow in gusts.

"Zees ees bad," LeMaire said. "Zee storm ees rolling een faster than expected."

I looked anxiously at Captain Hennessy. "Shouldn't we get to *Delilah*? We aren't pirates."

Without answering, Captain Hennessy rose and looked out the window again. I saw him ball his hands into fists.

"Sum bitch!"

He slid back down. I could see a mix of anger and fear swirl in the captain's eyes.

"What is it?" I asked him.

"We got problems."

"What? What problems?"

Captain Hennessy's face wrinkled into a grave, serious glare.

"They took Mac."

———

"ARE we just going to sit here?" I asked.

Minutes passed while LeMaire and Captain Hennessy spoke.

"Zay 'ave a camp downriver but zere ees no dock an' no way to sneak around. A smaller boat might get close enough but zat is *très risqué*."

"Risky, huh." Captain Hennessy huffed. He saw my urgent look. I felt my face sag and my eyebrows furrow in his gaze. "Mac's all we got an' I ain't gonna leave 'im."

The raid, if that's what it was, ended as quickly as it began. Thunder rumbled in the distance, but the Swampside Gang was gone.

I walked outside with Captain Hennessy and LeMaire. Men and women emerged from their hiding places and began to pick up the mess left behind. Carts had been upended. Two men lay wounded on the ground. Looking closer, I saw the man whose story of Belle Manor had spooked me. He lay on the ground as well, legs and arms sprawled apart like he had frozen in the middle of making a snow angel. There may have not been any snow today, and I could not say if his final destination was to be among angels, but the man was dead, nonetheless. Even from a distance, I could see his blank stare. His mouth hung open. His jagged, blackened teeth jutted out of his mouth in a final, morbid cry. Was he calling for help, cursing the men, or warning them that their deeds would see them an end such as those who haunted Belle Manor?

The good news, if any, was that they had gone. Captain Hennessy walked with long, purposeful steps to *Delilah*. I kept up the best I could, jogging at times to match his pace. LeMaire joined him in the lead. I hopped onboard behind the men and followed Captain Hennessy. He stopped abruptly at the outer cabin door, whirling around to give me one specific task.

"Run back and see if you can pick up their trail. Look for horse prints, cart tracks, footprints. Anything that will tell me which direction they were headed."

I did not ask questions, though I thought I had already heard LeMaire say he knew where the Swampside Gang's camp was located. I turned, hopped onto the dock, and ran as fast as I could to the dirt road that ran beyond Belle Manor in one direction and between the docks and the trading post in the other. I slid to a stop in the middle of the road and looked at the ground.

"Whatcha looking for?" a young voice said.

I looked up and saw the little boy that had taken shelter from the gunfire in the trading post with his mother. She was back at work as if nothing had happened, peddling produce, and trying to attract customers. The boy was out roaming around like it was Sunday afternoon.

"I said…"

"I heard you," I said. "I'm looking for tracks."

"Why?" The little boy skipped over to me.

"My friend was taken, and I'm gonna help get him back."

"Ohhh. If the Swampside Gang took him, he ain't comin' back. They'll either hang 'im or sell 'im."

This kid's honesty was not helping one bit. The thought of Mac hanging was not an image I wanted to have in my head. The other was just as bad, though given the choice, I'd rather be sold than killed.

"Was he a river pirate?" he asked.

I stopped looking for tracks and glared at the boy. "No!"

"Well, if'n they don't kill 'im, he's one now."

"What are you saying. I thought the gang got rid of river pirates."

"That's what they want everyone ta think. They're bad men, all of 'em. They only say they're after river pirates so's people look the other way. I know'd the troof."

"Do you know where they camp?"

"Uh-huh. But you better not go there, or you'll have ta be a river pirate, too."

I had to think fast. I glanced back at *Delilah* and saw Captain Hennessy moving about the deck. LeMaire was with him, but he did not seem to be helping. Feeling the stalk of sugarcane in my back pocket, I turned back to the boy and pulled it out for him to see.

"Look. Show me where they went, and I'll give you this."

I dangled the sweet treat in front of him like I was teasing a dog. His eyes bulged and I could tell his taste buds had been activated just by looking at what I was offering. He looked over his shoulder toward his mother, then back at me. He licked his lips, then pressed his pointer finger to his mouth.

"I know a shortcut, but we'll have ta be quick."

The boy took off running toward a large live oak tree growing on the opposite side of the road across from the docks. I started to follow him, then stopped and looked back at *Delilah*. For a moment, I thought Captain Hennessy saw me. I waved with both arms to get his attention, but he must have been looking elsewhere because he turned around without acknowledging me.

"Hey!" the boy yelled. "Ya comin'?"

What do I do? The longer I wait…Mac is in real danger.

Images of my father becoming surrounded by the band of men who ended up killing him flashed before my eyes. I watched from my hiding place without doing anything to help him. Why didn't I do something. Why!

Something in me clicked. It was like a fire had been set in the pit of my stomach, fueling me like the boiler that churned *Delilah's* secret weapon. The hotter it felt, the more I became determined to do something. Anything. I reached into the front pocket of my trousers and felt the steel of my brother's folding knife safely tucked away. Words from deep inside called out to me, "What are you?"

Without a second thought, I whirled around and ran at top speed to catch up to the boy. Together, we darted under the massive branches of the live oak tree and headed down a hidden path away from Captain Hennessy and the safety of Bayou Belle.

———

WE RAN through brambles and hopped over logs. At one point, we trudged through a marshy mix of mud and fallen leaves. With each sloshy step, I knew if I was going to see my first alligator, it would be somewhere in the muck we were in.

We came to a dry patch of earth that was reminiscent of a sandbar in the river and paused to catch our breath. Looking around I saw a deeper pool of water to one side. Ripples moved across the water as if something swam just below the surface. To the opposite side was an open draw of land. Oak trees with giant arms swinging about fought against the gusty winds that blew through them.

"Which way?" I asked.

The boy pointed to the trees. "Not much farther. The road bends around with the river. The Swampside Gang's camp is between the river and the road. Cuttin' across like we did was the short way, but nobody ever uses it."

"How come?"

"On account of all the alligators back there."

The hairs on my neck stood at attention as I looked back at where we had come.

"Now you tell me?"

"It weren't bad. Only saw three er four. It's the ones ya can't see that git ya."

Three or four, I thought. I did not see any.

The boy held out his hand. "Sugarcane? I ain't goin' no farther. If yer lucky enough ta git outta the camp, this is the best way back ta Bayou Belle."

"What's your name?" I asked.

"Gus."

I handed him the sugarcane, and he was off before I could ask any more questions.

"Great," I said to myself. "Now I'm alone with alligators on one side and the Swampside Gang on the other. I guess it couldn't get much worse."

Thunder clapped above me and I felt the cool drops of sprinkles start to accumulate on my skin. The wind howled through the trees, and once again, I was wrong.

———

MY FATHER USED to take my brother and me hunting. He taught us to track deer, wild turkey, and showed us how to snare rabbits using only what we could find on the land. The most important lesson he taught us was to become one with our surroundings. Feel the breeze and know it's direction, identify smells, keep our eyes peeled for signs of game, walk with light feet, leave no stone unturned, and always be aware of potential dangers that lurk nearby. We hunted in the wilderness, and there were plenty of animals that we were not after that could be hunting us. If we were able to master these skills, we would have a safe hunt and could successfully place ourselves in a position for an easy kill. While I was not hunting, I put those lessons to work as I crept forward beneath the trees and behind the taller grasses as I approached the road and the Swampside Gang's camp.

Just as Gus had said, the road followed the river around the bend then disappeared into the thickening brush of oak, bald cypress, and sweetgum trees. The trees lined the path, stretching their branches out creating a canopy that seemed to swallow the road. It looked like something out of a fairytale.

I squinted to keep the rain from getting in my eyes. From my hiding spot I could see a well-worn path that had been trampled over time by carts and horses that cut away from the road and headed for the river. My every sense was heightened, just as my father taught me. The wind blew from the south bringing with it the smell of damp soil, decaying leaves, and a salty taste that I had not experienced in rain before. In the direction of the river, I could hear voices shouting. Celebrating. Taunting. It was too far to make out the words, but it made my heart start to race just the same.

I took a deep breath and looked down the road in both directions. Seeing it was clear, I scampered from the cover of the tree to the entrance of the trampled path and hid in a tall mesh of grass. I crouched low, feeling the wet earth seep through my trousers, but I did not care. The sprinkles of misty rain were becoming heavier droplets of water that soaked into my clothes at first touch. I would be drenched in no time, so a soppy trouser leg was insignificant to me.

I paused for a moment to listen again. Feeling safe to move closer, I made my way along the edge of the path, keeping close to the tall grasses and smaller trees in case I had to dive for cover.

As I approached, the trees started to thin. I could see the dancing flames of a fire through the foliage. I slipped behind a large bald cypress, it's bark rough against my back, and peered around.

And there it was—the Swampside Gang's camp. A handful of tents were pitched around the fire. A few men milled about in the rain. I saw two younger boys about my age tending to the fire. Two other older men sat on stumps under tent tarps and cleaned weapons. From where I was it seemed that the rest of the gang had gathered around the base of a large oak near the banks of the Mississippi. Like the other oaks, it had many larger branches that drooped to the ground, but this tree towered above all others. The higher limbs swayed back and forth as if they were stranded and calling for help. One larger limb reached out over the water, bringing to mind a similar tree back home where I used to climb and leap into the river. The problem was that my tree was not a tool used for hanging men.

I watched in horror as the prisoner was forced toward the tree. His hands were bound behind him. He was beaten with sticks until he stood at the ancient oak's base. Two gang members sat above on the limb. When they saw that the prisoner was in place, they lowered a rope with a noose tied at the end. Without an explanation or opportunity for a final word, the noose was placed around the prisoner's neck, and cinched tight. The men on the branch each grabbed a handful of rope, and then, as if they were playing a game, leaped off the tree. Their combined weight lurched the prisoner into the air as they swung to the ground. Once on the ground, the Swampside men wrapped their end of the rope around the tree trunk and stepped back to watch as the rest of the gang whooped and hollered.

The prisoner's eyes bulged to look like frog eyes. His legs thrashed about. The skin of his neck bled from the tightened noose and his entire face turned bright purple. The force of the men who jumped from the tree was not enough to snap the prisoner's neck. Alone and terrified, he suffered his final moments of life in burning agony as his neck was stretched and the last of his breath was used up. He wiggled like a fish dangling at the end of a fishing pole. When finality struck, his legs stopped kicking and his body turned limp. Hung dead, he swayed back and forth in the wind like the tree branches above him.

Upon his death, the gang let out a cheer. The rope was released, and his body fell to the ground. The two men who had been in the tree removed the noose, then positioned themselves at either end of the dead prisoner's body. One grabbed his arms while the other grabbed his legs, and with an effortless heave, they tossed his body into the river.

My heart sank and surged all at once when I saw Mac tied with two other men to the base of a nearby oak. He was alive, but for how long?

I KNEW that I was in over my head, but with Mac's life on the line, I had to do something. I snuck closer. In my new position I had a clear view of Mac and could hear what was being said around camp. My fear for his life escalated when men with guns yelled out.

"Who will be the next man to meet the devil?"

I watched as two men with guns approached Mac and the two other remaining prisoners. One scratched and clawed at the tree behind him, fighting to slip free of the knots that held him. The other begged for his life.

"Please. Please! Not me. I'm no pirate. *I'm no pirate!*"

Mac sat quietly. His face looked solid as stone, expressionless, and his eyes remained focused as the men with guns decided who to hang next.

"Take him. Take the Black man."

The men shifted their attention to Mac. Still, he did not move a muscle.

"Yes, that's right. He's the one. Kill him."

It became clear that the man standing closest to the begging prisoner had heard enough.

"Shut up! Your whining will be the end of you!"

He rammed the stock of the long gun he carried into the side of the prisoner's head. I heard a sickening crack and watched the man tumble over. Blood erupted from a gash just above his left eye.

"Take him," the man said, wiping fresh blood from the end of his weapon.

The commotion drew the interest of the two boys who tended the fire. Together, they walked over to watch the next round of executions. I saw that the older men who sat cleaning weapons had a newfound interest as well. They turned their backs on the camp to watch the bloodied prisoner hang.

This is my chance, I thought.

Without a second to lose, I ran from my hiding place straight for the fire in the middle of camp. The rain continued to increase but had still not shown us its fullest intent. Lightning crackled and thunder rumbled. Gusts of wind sent sparks shooting across camp.

Sliding to a stop, I found a small, thin log in the fire that had an end poking out far enough for me to pull it free. My eyes darted left and right. I had a plan. With a torch in hand, it was time to set Mac free.

With a burst of speed, I ran behind the nearest tent. Using my knife, I cut a slit in the tent and peeked inside. I saw bedding, blankets, a half-empty bottle of whiskey, and a pile of dirty clothing tossed near the front flaps. I cut a longer strip in the backside of the tent and stepped through far enough to grab the bottle of whiskey. Exiting the tent, I poured some of the nasty-smelling booze on the roof and touched the flame on my torch to the mix of alcohol and tarp.

Flames took off like a fox chasing a jackrabbit. In no time, it engulfed one side of the tent. I had to move fast or risk being seen. I ran to the next tent, lit it, and scurried to the third and last tent in the row. The first tent was fully ablaze and the second was ramping up when I heard the crowd cheer. I peered around the third tent to see the begging prisoner swinging from his neck.

"Fire!"

I ducked behind the third tent. I heard men yelling. I had come this far and was determined to light the last tent. I poured the remainder of the whiskey on the tarp, cut a small slit in the tent, and lit the liquid fuel. With one quick motion, I pulled the slits apart and hesitated.

"Yes," I whispered, then tossed the burning log into the tent. I ran straight back from the burning camp to the cover of grass and a mix of trees with low-hanging limbs, then turned around to watch. I heard a sizzle come from the inside of the last tent. Crouching down, I covered my ears just in time.

BOOM!

The tent exploded in a tremendous ball of flame. Another explosion shook the ground, followed by another. The camp was a disaster. Men ran about unaware that they had been attacked only by one small boy. Some mounted horses. Others grabbed guns and ran toward the road.

In the commotion, I skirted the edge of camp, scraping and slicing my skin as I moved through a patch of sawgrass until I came to hide behind a tree only ten feet from Mac. I crouched low and looked around the tree. I saw the prisoner who was still tied with Mac pull frantically at his ropes in a desperate attempt to break free. Mac, on the other hand, looked me square in the eyes.

———

THE FIRES GREW despite the rain, spreading to whatever lay inside the tents. Tall, arching flames shot into the air. A crackling roar grew louder with each passing second as my distraction demanded the attention of everyone in camp. Everyone, that is, who was not running off to battle an invisible foe.

Adding the whiskey to act as fuel helped the blazes burn hotter. The flicker and flashes of jagged yellow and orange hues swirled together like a serpent taunting its prey. Men yelled for buckets to try and douse the flames, but they were fighting a losing battle.

Another explosion boomed from the third tent. Men who fought the fires dove for cover. Sparks and embers flew into the air. The smaller flaming shards burned out midflight but some of the larger ones found new places to grow again.

Thank God for gunpowder.

Black smoke billowed into the air, while a white haze blew across the ground. An awful smell spread, like the noxious odor of an old cigar, made it harder to breathe. Some men wrapped cloth around their faces. Others covered their mouths with their hands. As the fires raged on, the haze grew thick like an early morning fog, making it difficult to see. This was my chance. It was now, or never.

I ran from cover to the backside of the tree where Mac and the other man were tied. I removed my knife and sawed into the ropes that bound them. Rainwater dripped from my brow. The rope was spongy, making it harder to cut. The man tied with Mac spoke to himself in frantic bursts between smoke-agitated coughs, though I could not understand his foreign words. Mac remained calm, never once turning around.

The rope frayed bit by bit, until at last, I cut through. The frantic man yelled in triumph as if he thought his attempts to free himself were what caused their bindings to fall slack. He wriggled his wrists as if swatting at a swarm of bees until he was free of the tangles. Mac did not overreact and slipped free of the ropes, joining me behind the tree.

"We mus' goh, fas'!"

Mac started for the river.

"Wait! That's not the way. I know a shortcut that will get us back to *Delilah*."

"Dee men weel come back soon."

"Mac," I said, staring him in the eyes. "You saved me from the river. Trust me now to save you. I owe you."

The man who had been tied with Mac was so excited to

break free that he ran in the wrong direction through the haze toward the center of camp. He must have been seen because someone yelled out that a prisoner was getting away. Shots erupted from the camp. I could see shadows in the smoky mist as men from the Swampside Gang ran after their escapee.

As attention turned from fighting the fire to chasing the man, Mac had to make a decision to trust me, or take our chances going a direction neither of us knew to be right.

"Go," he said. "I weel follow."

I turned and ran back the way I came. Mac was on my heels, bent over, and running as low to the ground as possible. The wind swept the smoke in our direction. It was the perfect cover, but it made it extremely hard to breathe. I could hear men yelling to one another to return to camp. Another said to "spread out," and, "find the prisoners."

I hated to run back through the sawgrass, but there was no other way. We slipped into the sharp blades, added a few fresh stinging reminders across my hands and arms, and skirted the camp as we made our way for the road.

With a thunderous clap, the storm announced that it was no longer going to simply soak everything beneath but thrust a massive force upon us the likes of which I had never experienced. The wind blew harder, and the rain began to pour. The white haze that had been sailing with the wind now found itself no match for the extreme weather that was descending upon us.

Shots rang out from across the camp.

"We got 'im!" someone shouted.

Mac and I stopped to look and listen behind a cluster of tree branches. Hearing the men cheer gave me a momentary sense of false security, but I knew better.

"Where's the other?" another man yelled.

I glanced at Mac over my shoulder. His eyes looked intense as he crouched behind me.

"When we get to the road we have to cross into the trees on the opposite side. There is a trail. It's not much, but if we can make it there, we should be able to get back to Bayou Belle unnoticed."

"Where ees dee captain?"

"Last time I saw him, he was onboard *Delilah* talking with the man from the trading post."

"Come. Dare ees not much time."

Under the cover of the storm, what was left of the lingering smoke, and amid the confusion from the camp, Mac and I were able to forge our way through the taller grasses and behind the trees to a spot just shy of the main road that ran to and from Bayou Belle. Following Mac's lead, I dropped to my chest and crawled forward next to him.

"Where ees thees trail?"

I looked ahead. Everything seemed so similar. The voices around us were getting louder. Closer. Mac grunted, then looked behind us.

"Back to de reever," he said.

"No." I pointed at a tree with limbs that hung low enough to the ground, it looked as if it were opening its arms to us. "There. Just beyond that tree."

We crawled forward until my hands touched dirt. The road! I looked left and right, then locked eyes with Mac.

"Run!"

Lightning crackled overhead. Thunder roared. The rain came down in sheets, prickling my face as we ran. It took only a matter of seconds to cross the road and disappear into the brush. We slid to a stop to take a quick look behind us. I saw a group of men with their backs to us walking in the direction of the trampled path that led to the heart of the Swampside Gang's camp. Two more men walked behind the group at their own pace, falling farther behind with each lack-adaisical step.

"This way, Mac," I said turning for the trail that little Gus had shown me.

I had run only three steps when I startled a cloud of blackbirds taking shelter from the storm under the canopy of tangled tree branches. They scattered in a cacophonous burst of urgent chatter. Their vocal outburst and rustling of flapping wings from the trees alerted the last two men to our position.

"Geet up! Goh. GOH!"

Mac's voice was low, yet harsh enough to feel. I jumped to my feet, looking over my shoulder as I ran. Behind Mac, I saw that the men were after us. To my surprise, they did not alert the others.

"Watch where you ahr goeeng."

Mac was focused. I was not. I faced the front and led him deeper into the marshy swamp. The water level had risen considerably since I first crossed through with Gus. It slowed our escape. My feet felt heavier as I sank into the mud with each step. Water and sludge and dried leaves covered my knees, but there was no stopping. If we were to survive, I had to lead Mac out of the marshy mess we were in.

"Stop!" one of the men yelled from behind.

"Keep goeeng," Mac said. "Dey 'ave no guns. Only knives."

Only knives?

I squinted my eyes and placed my palm across my forehead to shield my vision from the rain. I could see the edge of the marsh.

"Almost out of the muck, Mac," I said.

Behind us, I saw movement in the water. I looked and saw what I thought was a fallen log floating nearby in the marsh. I began to turn my attention away from the log when it opened its eyes. *Alligator!* Captain Hennessy said I would see one. So did Gus. I never thought that when I finally saw an alligator that I would be in the water with it instead of looking down on it from the safety of *Delilah*. Appearing from the murky water next to the first alligator, a second emerged.

With sloppy steps, I felt the burn in my muscles. We had moved quickly through the bog, but the Swampside men were catching up to us. The constant hum of the rain impacting the trees and the water muffled all other sounds, but it did nothing to dampen the high-pitched scream behind us.

I stopped and whirled around. Mac bumped into me, knocking me off my feet. I sank to my neck in the water. With one muscular yank, Mac gripped my collar and pulled me to my feet in time to see one of the Swampside men thrashing about in the mouth of an alligator.

The second man jumped back as the alligator gnashed its jaws. Wet garbles of terrified pleas pierced the air. The shrill nature of the man's dying plight fell silent when the alligator began to roll. It twirled over and over like a barrel rolling down a hill. Water splashed with violent spats of killer instinct as the alligator tenderized its meal.

The second man staggered back, caught up in what looked like the shock of his life. Was he friends with the man who was being eaten? He cursed the alligator. He screamed what I assumed was the other man's name.

"Phillip! PHILLIP!"

I could not help but hear Gus's voice in my ear, "It's the ones ya can't see that git ya."

Mac placed his hands on my shoulders and turned me away.

"Goh," he said.

Though the thrashing had stopped, I could not help but feel the deadly ripples fall over my shoulders and down my spine. With a final step forward, we climbed out of the muddy bog and continued through the dark, wet bayou groves.

My side ached from running, but I had no choice but to

press on. Mac and I were drenched with salty-tasting rain, and rotten, muddy marsh water, but we had not been caught and were very close to Bayou Belle.

Wind whipped at us from all directions. Lightning flashed overhead, striking a nearby tree, spitting its branches with a hair-raising crack. I ducked as I ran. Twenty paces farther and I held my hands out for us to stop.

"Look, Mac. Can you see?"

"I see," he said.

Beyond the tree line was the road. Beyond the road was the trading post. And standing in front of the trading post with the long rifle in his hands, was Captain Hennessy. He looked to be arguing with his friend, LeMaire.

"Come, we can make eet."

I took a deep breath, but before we began to run, Mac placed his powerful palm on top of my head.

"Tank you," he said.

I looked up at him. His eyes were still intense, but I saw a glimmer of acceptance in his face. The power I felt from words so simple surged through me. I was tired, but I knew we were going to make it.

"You're welcome, Mac," I said. "Let's git while the gitten's good."

Mac grunted. I grunted back. A smile crept its way onto my face as we ran out of the trees. I wanted to yell out to Captain Hennessy. I wanted to jump for joy, but I knew that we would not be completely safe until we were onboard *Delilah* and moving away from Bayou Belle.

As we ran across the road, I saw Gus helping his mother push their cart toward Belle Manor. They fought the wind and rain as they trudged along. I waved once, but Gus did not see me. He held on to the cart with both hands and never looked my way.

LeMaire was the first to see us. He grabbed Captain Hennessy's arm and pointed at us. Instead of running over to greet us, he turned to LeMaire. The two men grasped each other's shoulders and shook each other once as if saying farewell.

Closing the distance, I thought Captain Hennessy would meet us. Instead, he waved one arm over his head, then pointed to the dock. He took off running as fast as his old legs would carry him. He had a sizable head start, reaching *Delilah* well before we did, and motioned to the dock workers to untie the lines.

No sooner had Mac and I made it halfway to the docks, that we heard men shouting in the distance. The storm muffled what they said, but a glance over my shoulder as we ran revealed four men on horses riding in our direction. They each had rifles and looked to be pushing their horses to run harder by the second.

One of the men aimed his rifle and fired. The bullet was not even close, but the sound of the blast still scared me to death. Another shot rang out. This one came from the docks. I saw Captain Hennessy on board *Delilah* with his rifle in hand. He fired again. White smoke appeared, then wafted away in the wind as the bullet soared through the air. I dared not look back for fear I might slow down or misplace a step and fall. Another blast chased after us but missed.

Our stride had been quiet as we ran across the dirt, so the hard knock and creak of wood beneath our feet signaled we were close to home as we hopped onto the dock and sprinted for *Delilah*.

On deck, I could see smoke puffing out of an exhaust pipe, which could only mean one thing. Captain Hennessy had fired up the boiler and was preparing to use our secret weapon, this time to help us escape.

We ran past the dock workers who had unmoored *Delilah*. They had taken cover from the gunfire behind two barrels on the dock. With Captain Hennessy at the helm, he had already begun to pull away as we approached. Without hesitation,

Mac and I jumped off the dock and landed on *Delilah's* deck, but we were not yet safe.

"To your posts!" Captain Hennessy ordered.

Mac grabbed his push pole and helped position *Delilah's* bow away from the docks. I did not yet have a job that would be useful at a time like this, so I stood near Captain Hennessy and waited for orders should he have any for me.

The Swampside Gangmen on horses had stopped at the river's edge and looked prepared to fire on us when a group of men led by LeMaire charged them from behind. Shots rang out, and the men on horses fell. I saw Captain Hennessy raise a hand and give a single wave. LeMaire answered in like fashion.

"Captain…" I started to say.

"Later, son. Things 'er a bit too rowdy right now ta be answerin' questions."

I stood in curious silence as we continued to pull away from Bayou Belle into a river that seemed to be flowing in the wrong direction. In fact, looking back toward shore, the river had risen so that the water level was almost even with the dock boards. I had been so concerned with running to *Delilah*, I did not notice the difference until now.

We churned into the river and headed back upstream. I felt that we were all safe from the Swampside Gang, but I could tell by the look on Captain Hennessy's face that we were not out of danger.

The wind blew harder than I could have ever imagined. I looked behind us. I could see Bayou Belle to one side. Belle Manor stood like an apparition on the hill. From the river, the columns looked like teeth in a massive skull and the windows portrayed the most evil of blackened eyes. It was a creepy sight, but it was nothing compared to what I saw closing in from downriver.

Lightning flashed and thunder rolled. The winds howled like a banshee on dark winter's night, but the river itself looked to have disappeared. I could not tell where the clouds ended and the river began, and a grayness within it all was closing in like a wall of water ready to crest over us all.

I tugged Captain Hennessy's arm.

"What is that?"

Mac ran from his spot at the bow to join Captain Hennessy and me. We churned as fast as *Delilah* could cut through the water, but it did not seem like it was going to be fast enough.

"That is God reminding us that we pale in significance compared to Him. That, my boy, is a hurricane."

The Return of Peter Jackson

Jackson

Ken Pratt

1

PETER JACKSON LEANED AGAINST THE RAIL OF THE MODEST stern-wheeler named the *Northern Wanderer* as it approached the coastal port of Astoria, Oregon. Peter had seen port cities all over the world built in bays or at the mouth of rivers; however, he had never seen a complete city built on a pier stretching out over the tidal flats quite like the city of Astoria was. The entire town was built on pilings, making it the largest pier in America.

The wind howled as it blew the rain down sideways in a heavy deluge under the dark skies of a stormy day. The other folks on the stern-wheeler were taking cover inside, but Peter was a sailor and foul weather didn't seem to bother him as he remained content on the deck. His wool coat, trousers and cap pulled down over his neck-length brown hair kept him warm and dry for the most part. He had paid for his passage from Portland and enjoyed the casual ride down the Willamette and Columbia Rivers to Astoria. He was glad to see several schooners anchored, waiting for their turn to moor their ship to the pier. Peter had worked on several sea-bearing vessels over the years and was an experienced shipwright. He doubted he would have much trouble finding work on one of the vessels already in port.

When the *Northern Wanderer* moored and the gangway was lowered, he walked purposely off the vessel onto the pier. While others hurried to escape the hard rain, he stood scanning his surroundings. He breathed in the salty air with a hint of freshly caught fish while the rain drops stung his cheek. He chuckled slightly as the blustering wind blew a man's derby hat off his head and carried it across the decking and over the edge into the Columbia River. It was exhilarating to be back near the open sea.

"Can I help you, sailor?" a man asked, noticing him standing idle in the weather.

Peter nodded slightly. "I'm looking for a sailor house for the night."

"Got a few. O'Grady's is three blocks south; Bishop's Cavern is a block farther and O'Donnel's is east a block."

Peter nodded appreciatively. "I have an old pal in town. Do you know a man named Nino Moore?"

"Nino? Yeah. He owns Nino's Restaurant over on Second Street. Great man."

Peter's lips rose to a smirk. "Yeah, he is." He nodded his thanks and stepped across the heavy beam decking to go farther into a crowded town built upon the pier's decking. He stopped at a cross street and watched two young teenagers walk past with large smiles and the sound of youthful laughter rang in his ears. Peter had no idea what the young friends were talking about, but the life they knew was trouble free and filled with youthful adventure. He remembered what it was like to be young and to believe life would always be as fun and exciting as it was in his youth. Little did he know back then how the troubles ahead would change him and that simple act of free-spirited laughter would fade away like a forgotten tin can decomposing at the bottom of the ocean.

Peter turned his attention from the two boys to continue his search for Nino's Restaurant.

Two blocks over, he entered Nino's. The restaurant was decorated with nautical ropes, netting, and a stuffed seagull or two mounted on a piece of driftwood. The restaurant was clean, bright and filled with the pleasing aroma of baked bread with a lingering scent of cooked fish that made his stomach growl with hunger. He questioned a waitress, "Is Nino here?"

The waitress, a lady in her midthirties, peered at him hesitantly before answering with a kind smile. "He's off today. But he'll be back tomorrow morning."

Despite his growling stomach, Peter left the restaurant to find a tavern for a needed drink. He found one not too far away and ordered a shot of stout whiskey at the bar. It didn't take more than a moment for a grizzled old man to join him, and ask, "What lady did you come off?" He had few teeth and appeared to have sailed around the world a dozen times while living hard in every port he visited.

Peter had no interest in talking. "The *Northern Wanderer*."

"Where's she call home?"

"I'm guessing Portland. I don't feel like talking." His cold eyes glared at the old-timer warningly.

"Enough said." The grizzled old man turned away to find someone else to talk to.

Peter looked at himself in a mirror behind the bar and didn't recognize himself for a moment. He had aged quite a bit in the years of sailing in the salty air and sun of the open ocean, along with the added stress of several fights and close calls with an angry sea. He looked ten years older than he was and now wore a dark beard and mustache to hide the scar of a sliced throat and cheek. He had been poked, stabbed, and sliced with a knife more times than he could remember, but on the same token, he had done his share of slashing and stabbing, too. There was a time when he was very much like the two young boys he had just witnessed joking and laughing together moments before. Now, as he peered at his reflection in a mirror, he appeared cold, mean and dangerous. He was nothing like the young man he used to be.

Every scar has a story, some more interesting than others. Peter looked at his hand holding the shot glass and stared at a scar on his wrist. The scar was the closest to a personal friend he had. Peter had seen the scar every day of his life since he was eight years old. Mad at his brother, Peter tried to hit him, but Phillip ducked and Peter's fist went through the window. Bleeding like heavy rain pouring off the roof wasn't enough to save him from the consequences of his father's wrath. Hitting the glass window had cut Peter's hand, but the damage was done and the window remained broken long after his cut had healed. Scars remained, too, and he had his share.

2

"THIS IS IT. WHAT DO YOU THINK?" PETER HAD ASKED WITH AN excited grin. He was twenty years old and worked as an apprentice at the local newspaper. He was inspired to be a journalist but began his career working in the print shop. He had finally paid off the engagement ring he wanted to give his sweetheart when he proposed. He was revealing it to his best friend, John Hackworth.

John took the ring in his fingers and gazed at it. It was a mere gold-plated band with a tiny diamond in the center. "I think when we make a fortune ferrying people across the river, you can buy Ellen a much larger diamond ring. But this one will do for now. Are you asking her tonight?"

Peter nodded. "I plan to."

"Well, if she says *no,* can I have the ring? I'd like to give it to Miss Sarah," John teased. John had grown up with Peter and they'd always been best friends. John worked at the granary on the Willamette River where he'd watch the steamboats hauling passengers and goods up and down the river. He had noticed a need for a ferry service across the Willamette near their town instead of traveling miles to reach the nearest one. He had plans to partner with Peter and make their fortune ferrying people across the Willamette.

Peter had laughed. "If she tells me *no*, I'll probably throw the ring into the privy with my hopes of marrying her. You could jump in there and dig for it, though. If you find it in that muck, you can have it."

"She isn't going to reject you, Peter. She loves you far too much for that. I'll have to buy my own someday when Sarah realizes that I'm alive."

Peter chuckled. "You just met Sarah. Give her a chance to get to know you."

PETER STROLLED through the heavy rain with his memories of John. Peter had recently gone to the spot along the Willamette River where John wanted to build a ferry, but nothing was there. Peter sat beside the river for a while, remembering the many talks and dreams of building a ferry there. That particular spot on the river was their summer swimming hole and where Peter had asked his sweetheart, Ellen Whittaker, to marry him. There might've been more romantic places to ask her, but on a hot summer evening, the cool sandy riverbank seemed as nice as any place.

Some memories were more painful to recall than others. Ellen Whittaker was the only girl Peter had ever loved. She was seventeen and in Peter's eyes, she was beautiful with light brown hair and the loveliest blue eyes a young lady could have. They had been courting for two years and were neighbors; their families were close friends. There wasn't a girl anywhere else in the world that could pull Peter's eyes off Ellen. She was his lady, and no one could change that. Peter had his future planned out and would become a successful journalist and half-proprietor of the Hackworth and Jackson Ferry. His future goal was to start his own newspaper. And through it all, Ellen would be his beautiful wife who would always be right by his side and partner in everything he did. What a life it could have been if dreams came true.

A strange pressure compressed against Peter's chest as he remembered the moisture that filled Ellen's eyes when he got down on one knee in the soft sand of the river's bank.

"Will you marry me?" he asked with enough butterflies inside him that he thought he might be able to fly if she agreed.

Ellen's mouth dropped open with surprise. Her blue eyes clouded with thick tears as a smile lifted her lips into a grin. "Yes. Yes! Oh, Peter, yes!" She leaped forward and knocked him down into the sand with a kiss that would have outraged her parents if they'd witnessed it.

"We're going to be so happy!" she said. "I love you, Peter Jackson! Of course, I'll marry you."

Peter had stood in that exact spot and wished he could go back in time to relive it again and again. If there was any one particular time where he was happiest, it was there within that moment. That one moment in time with Ellen would never be surpassed as the greatest moment of his life.

3

AFTER A FEW DRINKS AT THE TAVERN, PETER RETURNED TO Nino's Restaurant to get something to eat. He had not eaten since the day before and the smell of freshly baked bread and buttered fish had left a terrible hunger that liquor couldn't fill. He found a table in the corner to sit quietly and order lunch.

"Peter? Is that you?" A man asked, approaching him slowly, inquisitively. "Oh, my word, it is! How are you? Do you remember me? Otto Davidson."

Otto Davidson came aboard the *King's Desperation*, an Irish schooner named in honor of the queen by the vessel's owner, who wasn't too fond of the British reign over Ireland. Otto was a greenhorn deckhand, sixteen years old and full of fire and vinegar, who wanted to work his way up to be a captain and have his own ship someday. The *King's Desperation* primarily sailed the European trade routes through the Mediterranean, Atlantic, and North Seas. A cargo of goods being shipped to the Port of Marseille in France happened to coincide with the vessel's shore leave during the July 14th celebration of the Storming of Bastille Day.

Peter and the crew of the *King's Desperation* joined in with the celebration. Intoxicated, Otto said some unpleasantries to a few French women when they shunned his advances. Offended, the ladies told their husbands and before Peter and his fellow crew members knew it, they were confronted by a group of fired-up French soldiers who wanted a bit of their blood more than an apology. The *King's Desperation* crew were severely beaten up in a fight they could not walk away from. Angry and drunk, Peter pulled his knife and stabbed two men before slicing a third severely.

It was bad luck that Otto had insulted those particular ladies because the French government did not appreciate their soldiers' lives being threatened by an unruly American sailing on an Irish ship. Peter was the only one who pulled a weapon and was sentenced to three years of hard labor in the penal colony of French Guiana, otherwise known as Devil's Island.

If hell had a definition on earth, it would be the Devil's Island Penal Colony. Peter was sentenced to three years of hard labor in the hot tropical jungle and found he was more nourished by the weevils in the food than the food itself. The guards were hardened to the plight of the convicts and some guards took pleasure in beating the convicts for the slightest infraction or weakness in a moment of exhaustion during the hellish workday. Every day was a day that Peter had to fight to survive; he fought prisoners, fought the humiliation of the guards, and fought disease repeatedly. To make his sentence just a bit harder, he was an American in a French prison and had to learn the language, and over time, he did.

French law demanded that prisoners who served their time and were freed still had to remain in French Guiana as free men for the same amount of time they were sentenced unless their sentence was eight years or longer; then, they had to stay there for life. That law turned Peter's three-year sentence into a six-year sentence.

Peter served one year of hell as a prisoner doing forced labor, but knowing he was an experienced shipwright, he was offered a life-altering proposition. A French merchant ship arriving in the French Guianas had struck a reef and needed an experienced shipwright immediately. As an experienced maritime carpenter, Peter was given the choice to serve the remainder of his time doing forced labor or joining the crew of a French merchant ship for the next five years. He would be sentenced to life on Devil's Island if he tried to escape the ship. He committed to becoming a French sailor and remained true to his commitment for the next five years.

At the end of his five-year sentence, Peter found work on an English cutter, returning to England. He then searched the piers for a ship going to Portland as the American and English wheat trade routinely went to Oregon's Willamette Valley and the Port of Portland. Peter's inquiries had found him a vessel needing a shipwright bound for Oregon and after nine long years, Peter came home.

"I thought you were dead," Otto said, joining Peter's table uninvited. "I never told you how sorry I am about that fight. It's good to see you."

Peter stared at Otto with no expression on his face. "Are you a captain yet?"

Otto shrugged. "First mate on an English bark. Give me three years and I will be. You?"

"Just a carpenter."

"I cannot believe it's you. We all thought you got the guillotine."

"It might've been nicer if I did. You started that fight, Otto. I don't hold you accountable for what I did, but it wouldn't have happened if you hadn't harassed those women. Their husbands were right there and in their soldier uniforms, cele-brating a holiday with their wives. They were leaving us alone, but you refused to leave them alone even after we all told you to."

"I said I was sorry…"

"I spent a year in pure hell, appropriately named Devil's

Island, fighting prisoners, the guards, venomous snakes, mosquitoes, leeches, malaria and every sickness that would come and go. I ate every worm, maggot and rotting fruit I could find to not starve to death and drop dead like many others. They had a guillotine, too, and I was almost to the point of forcing them to use it when I was sentenced to a French vessel to serve out my time. Five years without pay, but it got me out of that hellhole. I'll never know how that came about, but that's the only reason I'm alive. Many nights, I laid awake wondering why I was going through all that. It's because I was protecting you."

Otto moved his head back and forth just slightly. "I had no idea," he said. "Peter, I was a stupid kid. Sixteen and experiencing the world for the first time."

"Otto, I don't blame you for what I did; that's on me. Keep it in mind the next time you decide to harass women. The consequences may not be worth the effort when it's all said and done. For six long years, I paid for that one night because of a fight. It was a fight I tried to avoid, to begin with. You started it, knowing we would have to finish it because you couldn't fight your way through a blustery wind." Peter smiled slightly for the first time. "My life is always paying the price for somebody else's decisions. It's good to see you, Otto. I wish you well, but I'd like to finish my meal in peace."

"Of course. I am sorry. It is good to see you, old friend. Maybe we'll cross paths again."

"Perhaps." Peter shook the young man's hand and continued to eat his supper. *Old friend.* The phrase itself had meaning—a friend that used to be. He had several shipmates over the years and few were considered true friends. He had made a friend in prison named Sal, but he had watched Sal die, too. Of all the brutality on Devil's Island between the inmates, guards and work detail in the burning sun, it was a tiny mosquito that had killed Sal. Malaria did him in like it did thousands of others.

Otto turned back, and said, "Hey, I was in Marseilles and walked along the pier until I found those initials you carved into the decking, K.M. I thought of you and me sitting there with a bottle when you did that. She was your sweetheart, right?"

Peter nodded quietly.

"I'll see you in port somewhere. I still think of you, old friend. Take care," Otto said before joining his current shipmates.

Karl Musgrove is a name that was burned in Peter's memory and plagued him for the nine years he was away. Most men in prison might engrave their name or initials on the wall, their bunks, or wherever possible. Peter engraved the letters K.M. It wasn't a dedication of love like Ellen's initials might have been. The initials K.M. were a reminder of hate, the sole object that had seen Peter through much pain, sickness and sorrow. His greatest fear was not losing hope and dying like many on Devil's Island; it was forgetting the man's name that changed his life forever. Peter refused to die before he could kill Karl Musgrove.

4

THE DATE WAS SET. JUNE 17TH WOULD BE THEIR WEDDING DAY. He and Ellen attended the local church where the wedding would be held, and everything was ready. The excitement was exhilarating, and the future was so promising and filled with hope that nothing seemed to cast a shadow over the young couple.

John Hackworth was excited for his friend and gathered Phillip, Peter's brother, to take Peter to Portland for a night of fun and excitement before Peter married his bride.

"What will I do there that I can't do here? I don't drink and have no interest in other women, so what am I going for?" Peter had questioned Ellen. "I think it's silly. I would rather hoe weeds in the garden with you."

"You don't like gardening," she chuckled.

"I know. That's what I'm saying. I have no interest in going to the city to watch John and Phillip get drunk and act like fools. I'll be bored to death. I'd rather hoe the garden with you."

"Peter, John wants you to go. We're getting married and he knows your friendship will change. Your brother, too. He's really looking forward to going to the city for one last hurrah with you. Go have fun."

"Fun doing what?"

Ellen's brow lowered in thought. "Simply being with your best friend and brother before we get married. I know you don't drink, but you can still enjoy yourself. Promise me that you'll have one or two drinks with them and behave yourself. You'll all be coming home in the morning. They may not feel too well and you can have fun on the way home, reminding them why. But let them enjoy themselves and you do, too. Rachel and Sue will be here with me doing the same thing; we'll have tea and talk all night, maybe go to the river for a midnight swim."

"I'd rather do that."

"No. Now, get going. They are waiting for you."

"A kiss before I go?"

"Of course. But only a small one. The day after tomorrow, we will be husband and wife. And I cannot wait." She kissed him softly and walked him to the door. Outside, John and Phillip waited on horseback.

"Let's go! We have a two-hour ride, Peter!" Phillip shouted. "You can survive for one day without her."

"Oh, hush," Peter said as he stepped into the saddle of one of their farm horses. The Jackson farm wasn't too big, but they grew twenty acres of wheat, which helped keep them fed, and they had a solid roof over their head.

"Tonight, we have you to ourselves," Phillip said.

John added, "No women, no Ellen, no parents, cousins or aunts and uncles, heck, not even a neighbor to spread gossip about what we do. That, my friend, means you're drinking and will enjoy it!"

Portland was a city that provided just about anything that anyone could want. A cheap boardinghouse, cheap alcohol, and cheap food were about all the three friends were looking for and finding. They went to one tavern, then another and finally to a pub where Phillip had to excuse himself to go outside and vomit all he had drank from the previous stops. He was quite intoxicated when Peter and John walked him back to the boardinghouse and put him to bed. Deciding to go back for another drink before calling it a night, they walked into the pub. Running short of money, John made the loud announcement that Peter was getting married and welcomed any well-wishes or congratulations to be made by purchasing them a drink.

A man brought them two shot glasses from the bar, and said, "It's on the house. My name is Karl Musgrove. Mind if I join you?"

"Not at all, thank you!" John said, taking a shot glass and drinking it.

Karl shook Peter's hand. "Congratulations. I see you're not quite as drunk as your friend."

"I don't drink much. But thank you."

"Well, if I'm buying, you better drink. Once you're married, these moments may be far and in between." He turned around, and shouted, "Nino, keep the drinks coming over here. This man is getting married!"

"You got it, Karl!"

For the next hour, they drank until John passed out on the table. Peter had consumed a few shots, but the alcohol affected him more than he thought it would. Peter was barely conscious when four men helped John and himself out of the pub and down the street. The last thing Peter remembered was a stairway they were taking him down.

The following day, he woke in a groggy haze aboard a ship. He was tied up and John was nowhere to be found.

The captain came downstairs with the Articles of Agreement supposedly signed by him the night before. "I'm glad to see you're awake. You signed on with us in your drunken stupor and now are property of the *J.N.D. Horzen*. Once we reach the open sea, you can decide whether you want to remain on board. Until then, you'll wait here. Can I get you any water or food?"

"Where's John?"

"Your friend is dead. I'm guessing he was allergic to whatever he drank or had too much of it. I did him a favor and dropped him in the river. He'll be found and returned to his family, most likely."

"John's dead?" Peter asked, not comprehending the words or where he was, let alone what was happening. His head ached and throbbed.

"He is. You signed your name as Peter. Is that right?"

"I didn't sign anything. Wait…where am I? Who are you?"

"You are on my ship. You signed the Articles of Agreement and we're going to England."

"I shouldn't be here. This is wrong. I didn't sign anything. I'm getting married tomorrow. You have to let me off the ship, please. I'm getting married!" Peter shouted. He was beginning to understand the dire circumstances of his situation.

"Not anymore, you're not. You are a sailor now aboard our lady, the *J.N.D. Horzen*. Like I said, once we're at sea, your bounds will be cut and you will begin your new career or try to swim the five miles back to shore. Until then, you're free to scream, cry, or do whatever you want to do to get it out of your system. But you will obey and do as you're told or suffer the consequences, which I assure you, you do not want to do."

"Who signed my name!" Peter demanded to know.

The captain smiled. "You did. Just like John signed his."

"Was it Karl Musgrove?" Peter questioned.

"I don't know who that is, but I assume he is part of a press-gang that grabbed you. I purchased you from his boss, whose name I won't tell for any future needs. This is the last I want to hear about it. What is, is what it is. Get used to it. Good day."

Peter rubbed his beard as he stared at the empty bowl on

the restaurant table. The memory of being shanghaied was hard to swallow. The day he was supposed to marry Ellen, he was twenty miles out to sea and well over a hundred miles down the coastline heading to South America. By then the first mate's leather strap had been whipped across his back several times over the next few days as Peter struggled to learn about a world he knew nothing about. His crewmates belittled him, beat him, and humiliated him. He was the low man on the totem pole and, as such, got the worst work assignments and the least food, the worst blankets and bunk, and was harassed day and night. Life had become miserable and the constant threat of being tossed overboard by the captain and crew for even minor errors had become common-place. Gradually, he became a sailor and was accepted as a crewmate once he had shown some skill in carpentry and began working with the shipwright. He had a lot to learn, but given his choice between survival or death, he chose to learn all he could. He had become a sailor, though hidden inside his boots were the scratched initials K.M. just above a skull and crossbones.

A man can pray in church, but he can also pray at sea or in prison. Peter had prayed on foreign lands and everywhere else, but nothing had changed. *He* was the only thing that changed. Peter walked away from his Christian faith and learned how to kill with a knife. It was the weapon of sailors, and they all carried a knife. He had his share of knife fights and was not always the winner, but he had survived them all.

"Hello, I'm Reverend Hollman. Can I join you?" he asked Peter.

Peter shook his head. "No."

"Oh. Well, I'll sit right here at this table next to you. I am starving today. I see you had the stew. That's an excellent choice. Would you like another bowl or a piece of pie? I'll buy."

Peter looked at him with annoyance. "No."

"Very well. Let me ask, have you heard the Gospel of Jesus Christ?"

Peter nodded slowly. "I grew up in the church, Reverend. I've heard it all before and I never saw it help me. I have no interest in hearing it."

"I must confess I overheard your conversation with that other man and I am intrigued. You were sentenced to three years of hard labor in the French Guiana penal facility and then got to sail on a ship to finish a five-year prison sentence. And you still say the Lord did nothing for you?"

"What do you know about Devil's Island?"

"Nothing. I met a Frenchman once who was wanted for a crime he claimed he was innocent of and hopped aboard an English ship before he was arrested. He feared going there; he said it was a cruel place. Maybe the Lord has done more for you than you know."

"Maybe. But I haven't seen it, preacher."

"Are you looking?"

"The only thing I am looking for is the man who made me into a sailor so I can thank him in person. And when I find him, I'll do that."

"If he lives around here, maybe I can help. I have a church here in town, but I think of the sailor houses, taverns and pier as my mission field. Our paths might have crossed. Does this man have a name?"

"Nino Moore."

"Nino, yes. He owns this place; I know him very well. He and his family attend our church. Wonderful family."

"I bet," Peter said doubtfully. "I plan on visiting him."

"Oh, good. I'm sure Nino will be glad to see you."

Peter smiled bitterly. "I bet he will. Have a good day, preach."

5

It was a week before when the English bark the *S.S. Sir Elliot Burbank* docked in Portland. Peter collected his first substantial pay in six years and stepped onto Oregon soil for the first time in nine years. He paid for a bath and trimmed his beard before taking a stagecoach back to his hometown.

Peter was filled with excitement and anxiety about going home after so long. The town had not changed so much that it was unrecognizable but had expanded. The newspaper he had worked for expanded its building and was thriving. The granary where his father, brother, and friend John had worked thrived and grew along the river. Everything had grown a little bit bigger, even the church he had attended with Ellen.

He walked out of town to his family farm and knocked on the house's door, half excited and half afraid of seeing his parents when the door opened. He wondered how much they had aged or if they would recognize him now.

A child of about eleven opened the door. "Hello," the kid said with an intimidated voice as he stared at the unkept neck-length hair and bearded man dressed in black wool pants and coat with a wool cap pulled over his head. He carried a gray canvas bag with personal items.

Peter stared at the kid blankly. He had no idea who the kid may have belonged to. "Are your parents home?"

A lady appeared behind the child. "May I help you?"

Peter had never seen her before. "Um...Are Henry and Viola Jackson here?"

The lady shook her head. "The Jacksons don't live here anymore. We bought this place after Henry passed away."

Peter's breath was sucked out of his chest. His eyes began to water, and he couldn't speak as the words tore through his chest. "Passed away?" he questioned.

"Yes. Did you know them?"

He nodded silently. "Do you know where my mother is?"

The lady's expression changed empathetically. "Were they your parents?"

Peter nodded.

"I'm sorry. She passed before he did. I never knew them, but that is what I heard. Their son sold us this property."

"Do you know where Phillip is now?"

She shook her head. "I'm afraid I don't. We bought this place five years ago."

"What about my sister?"

She shook her head. "I know nothing about her."

"Thank you," Peter said. He tried to smile, but his heart was suddenly breaking like a bridge made of willow twigs bending under the pressure of the weight threatening to snap while he tried to hold himself together. He turned from the house he had grown up in and walked up the driveway for the last time. His parents and the home he had known were gone. He stepped along the same path he had walked so many times in his youth to the neighboring farm to see his fiancée, Ellen Whittaker. He stepped onto the porch and knocked on the door hoping the Whittaker family still lived there.

Ellen's mother opened the door. She had aged but looked the same. "Can I help you?" she asked.

Peter was thankful to see a face that he recognized, and a glimmer of hope rose within him that maybe Ellen had remained single all these years. He smiled despite the tears that clouded his eyes. "Missus Whittaker, it's me, Peter Jackson."

Her knees felt weak for a moment and she almost collapsed as her hand went to her breast, shocked to see him. "Peter?" she gasped.

He laughed slightly. "I'm home." He motioned toward his old house, his eyes clouding heavily with tears. "I just found out my parents are gone."

"Oh, my word!" Grace Whittaker gasped. She was about to invite him inside but hesitated. "You poor boy." Her eyes gazed at him with empathy and yet uncertainty. "Um…let me clean up my mess, and then I'll make you some lunch. Give me a moment," she said, and closed the door.

Peter glanced across a pair of fields to his parents' old home. How often had he stood on Ellen's porch to ask for her? The countless times came to mind of Ellen and him sitting on the porch swing talking until the moon was high in the night sky. His whole youth was invested between the two farms, and he could sit for hours and reminisce about his years growing up and courting Ellen.

He sniffled with excitement that Missus Whittaker might go inside to tell Ellen that her fiancé had returned. The hope of seeing his beautiful Ellen come to the door excited to see him brought a smile as he waited with an expanding hope. Peter had written Ellen letters but was never too confident they would reach her. If they did, then she would know he had promised to come home for her and if she loved him as he loved her, she would have waited for him. The longer he waited, the stronger the hope of seeing Ellen grew.

The door opened, and Missus Whittaker invited him

inside. "It's been so long, Peter. I am stunned. I cannot believe that you are here. Please have a seat. I got you a cup of coffee and a bit of cake. Where have you been?"

Entering the home, like standing on the porch, filled him with a deep sense of reminiscence. There was no place in the house where he did not remember Ellen standing or sitting. He had sailed the seven seas and there was no ocean depth that could compare to how deeply he loved her.

"I've been better. I was looking forward to seeing my parents…Um, I just heard."

"Yes. Your mother passed away sometime after you did. I mean, after you disappeared. We all thought you were dead after John's body was found in the river."

"They never got my letters? Ellen never got my letters?" Peter asked with a pain-filled expression.

She shook her head. "No."

Peter bit his bottom lip emotionally to hold himself together. He raised his hands dumbfounded. "Do you know where Phillip and my sister are now?"

Grace shook her head. "No. Phillip was devastated after…well, after John's body was found. They couldn't find yours."

He rolled his eyes emotionally. "I was shanghaied."

She exhaled sadly. "Phillip never got over the guilt and blamed himself. After your father passed, he sold the farm and left. I don't know where he went."

"My sister?"

"She left with Phillip. I believe Phillip wanted to get far away from Portland and the memories of what happened there, so they left the state."

"And Ellen? Did she think I was dead too?"

"Peter, please understand that we had nothing else to believe. There is a tombstone with your name on it next to your mother and father's. Your mother wanted to be buried next to you."

"I wasn't dead." He struggled to fight the tears that clouded his eyes.

"We did not know that."

He sniffled as the weight of the news weighed heavily on his chest. His voice trembled as he asked, "And Ellen? Did she marry someone else?"

Grace nodded once, slowly. "Yes."

Peter closed his eyes as a tear flowed free for the first time in so long that he forgot the last time a tear fell.

"Who?"

"A gentleman named Frank. They moved to Oklahoma."

"Well, I hope they are happy." He wiped his eyes. "I don't think I have anything else to say. Everyone I loved is gone."

"Peter, you're home now and that's something to be thankful for. You can start over somewhere else. There are a lot of jobs in Portland. The Lord didn't keep you safe and bring you back here for nothing."

He raised a single finger, hesitating to wait as he swallowed some coffee. "There's only one reason I can think of and that's to find the men that did this to me." He stood. "Missus Whittaker, give Ellen my love. And tell her, tell her I tried to get home." His eyes filled with moisture as he shook his head, and his lips snarled. "Good day."

"Peter, Ellen has a family and is happy. She loves her husband. Be happy for her."

"I am. I never wanted anything but good things for Ellen. I wish her well."

"It's not too late for you to find someone to love and be happy with. Peter, when you were young, you had a glimmer of joy in your eyes. Now, your eyes are still blue but cold like steel. I don't know what you've been through, and you have every reason to be angry, but you must forgive those who harmed you."

He chuckled bitterly. "Forgive them? No. I've lost nine years of my life and everyone I loved, including my family.

I'm finding the people responsible, but forgiving them is the last thing I will do."

"What you have in mind may only lead to prison. It's not worth spending your life in prison when you can accept what is, is the way it is. You can choose to invest in the rest of your life, moving forward, falling in love, and creating a good life and family. You have a chance to be happy and if you take it, maybe those warm and lively blue eyes I remember so well will return."

"I've already been to hell and back. It can't get much worse. It's good to see you, Missus Whittaker."

"Peter, please...let the past go and move on."

He chuckled bitterly. "There is already a tombstone with my name on it, apparently. It's hard to let the past go when it's etched in stone. Tell your daughter...tell Ellen, I understand and congratulations."

Peter stood in the cemetery staring at his parents' tombstones and his own. *Gone but not forgotten* was etched into his tombstone. There was only one word to describe the emotion that filled him to see his own gravestone beside his parents'— haunted. It symbolized the end of his life, yet he was alive and well, standing before the very symbol that ended his existence. There was a desperation to let his brother Phillip and sister know that he was alive and had come home. But, like reaching out to his parents, there was no way to know where his brother and sister were. He knew where his parents were —they were in heaven—but his siblings could be anywhere. If he could, he would tell Phillip how lucky he was to have gotten sick that night and to be thankful for it. Peter had always been thankful for it. He would tell Phillip he was grateful to still have a brother back home.

To find his siblings, Peter went to the newspaper he used to work for and spoke to one of the reporters to tell his story and to ask them to try to find Phillip and his sister. Along with asking them to have his tombstone removed because, despite his disappearance, he was, after all, alive.

6

KARL MUSGROVE HAD READ THE NEWSPAPER ARTICLE TITLED "A Dark Homecoming for Peter Jackson." Karl had come far since those days of patrolling the streets and piers with his few friends, guiding drunken sailors to a specific sailor house for the night or when needed, taking young men like Peter Jackson and his friend, John, off the street. Unfortunately, Peter's friend John had an allergic reaction to the drug being used, but since both young men were unconscious, the ship's captain paid the same amount for both bodies. Karl got his cut and that was all he cared about.

In the past nine years, Karl had risen from a street hood to one of the more prominent crimps in the city. After months at sea, sailors coming to port were anxious to get to shore to drink, carouse and find a bordello. All of which were provided free of charge to the sailor while staying at one of the three sailor houses that Karl owned. However, nothing was free. The sailor accrued a heavily inflated debt; when a ship needed a crew, the captain paid the sailor's debt, which the sailor would then have to work off by going to sea. Ships entered and left Portland daily, and the business of brokering sailors had made Karl a very wealthy man.

Karl dressed well, lived well and now had all the authority over his press-gangs to do his dirty work while he kept his hands clean doing a legitimate business. Only when needed did his hired men drug unsuspecting men to be shanghaied like Peter Jackson was.

It was a cool and wet night when Karl opened the door to leave his house, expecting to meet a friend at the local tavern. He stepped out the door with a carefree whistle of a tune when a wooden club slammed against his face, shattering his nose upon impact. Karl stumbled back inside the house and fell to the floor, holding his bleeding and swelling nose. His eyes were filled with tears blurring his vision as he looked toward the door to see a dark figure dressed in black appeared out of the darkness and stepped into the house, closing the door behind him.

The man switched the club to his left hand and pulled his knife from the sheath under his jacket with his right hand. "Do you remember me?"

Karl immediately recognized who the man was. "It wasn't me! I'm not the one you want! I only did what I was told to do. I swear it!"

Peter's murderous expression was fierce and wild like a snarling wolf. "I've been waiting for this moment for nine years!"

In a panic, Karl tried to reach for the derringer in his pant pocket, but Peter swung the club, bashing it across Karl's wrist. Grabbing his injured wrist, Karl cried out desperately, "Listen! I was just the errand boy. Nino told me to drug you. Nino is the one who did it!"

"Who is Nino?"

"Moore. Nino Moore. He was in charge. I just did what I was told. It was all him, not me. I swear it!"

"Who forged my name on the Articles of Agreement?"

"Nino did! Nino is who chose and sold you and your

friend, not me. All I did was hand you the drinks! He's the one you want, not me."

"Where can I find Nino?" Peter questioned while leaning over Karl.

"Astoria! He's living in Astoria. Please…" Karl began to whimper. "Wait! Listen, he took your…"

Peter plunged the knife into the side of Karl's neck without a moment's hesitation. "I'll kill him too, but this is for killing John." He ripped the blade upwards, slicing through the tissue and opening Karl's throat in a wide gash that bled like a bucket being poured out onto the floor. Peter stood watching until Karl was dead. Nine years of waiting for the moment at hand still left no satisfaction; there was more man to kill. A man he'd never officially met, named Nino Moore.

7

PETER LEFT NINO'S RESTAURANT AND STEPPED OUTSIDE INTO THE blustery wind and rain. He needed to find a sailor's house to stay the night. He knew Nino Moore would be at the restaurant in the morning. Once he met Nino, he could follow him home and find the right moment to cut the man's throat before disappearing at sea.

A store door opened, and a woman holding her daughter's hand entered the weather. She was wearing a heavy parka with a fur-lined hood over her head. She bent down. "Let's button your hood, Joanna." She stood and turned around, almost running into Peter. "Oh, excuse me," she giggled. She looked at Peter's face for just a second as he stepped around her.

"Sorry, Miss," Peter said as he stepped around the six-year-old child and kept walking.

The woman froze and turned back toward him. "Peter?"

He heard his name and turned around at the sound of the voice. It was like a ghost from the past.

The woman pulled the hood off her head to reveal her face. "Peter, is that you?"

"Ellen?" he could not believe his eyes. Ellen Whittaker was standing in front of him.

"My gosh. Peter. It is you. Where…How…?"

His vision clouded with moisture. "Your mother said you lived in Oklahoma."

"Oklahoma? No. I live here in Astoria." She peered at him in disbelief. "I thought you were dead."

He shook his head, yearning to grab hold of her and pull her close. "I'm not. I was…"

The store's door opened, and a man came out and put his arm around Ellen. "Hello," he said protectively to Peter.

"Hon, this is my old friend, Peter Jackson! I just ran into him. This is unbelievable! Peter, this is my husband, Nino."

Nino held out a hand to shake. "Oh. Nice to meet you, Peter."

Peter's spine straightened with a cold chill that sent a wave of rage through him. His right hand moved forward to shake the man's hand that had ruined his life and now somehow stole his future, too. He squeezed Nino's hand forcefully. Nino matched the strength of the grip. Peter's eyes held on Nino's like a jaguar stalking its prey.

Ellen said, "Peter, we must have you over for dinner. Are you in town for long? Are you free tonight? I'm just making a beef stew, but there will be plenty. Please join us. You don't mind, do you, Nino?"

Nino pulled his eyes off Peter with a soft smile. "No. Not at all. It would be nice to get to know your old friend." Nino would not have recognized Peter, but the article about Peter spread across the country and made it in today's Astoria paper. Nino had read the article and tossed the paper into the woodstove to hide it from Ellen. Earlier that morning, he had gotten a wire that his old friend Karl Musgrove had been murdered. It was not by coincidence that Peter was in Astoria and Nino knew precisely why the man was here. It was safer to invite him to his family home than to meet him on the street.

Peter was speechless.

"Peter, please?" Ellen asked again.

"Your mother said you married a man named Frank," he said.

"Franklyn Nino Moore, yes. I'm Ellen Moore now. This is our oldest daughter, Joanna. We also have a son named John. *Johnathon Peter*," she emphasized with an empathetic smile. "He's named after you and John. Please come to dinner."

Peter looked at Nino. "Alright. When and where?"

"Tonight. Say, six o'clock?"

8

Nino had provided for Ellen well, as they lived a short way up the hill in a large three-story home. It was a beautiful house with a well-groomed yard and a wide covered porch overlooking the river and pier. It was easy to imagine how nice it would be to sit on the porch on a warm summer's evening with a glass of sun tea and enjoy the view.

"Oh, my goodness," Ellen said emphatically. "What kind of monsters would do that to you? We thought you were dead. It was the saddest time of my life. Phillip had spent hours looking for you two and he was so broken afterwards. It was a horrifying time."

They had eaten a nice dinner at the table and were now sitting in a large reading room to talk without the children having to hear. Ellen sat beside her husband on a small davenport while Peter sat in an oversized, padded chair, sipping coffee.

Ellen continued, "Do you know who shanghaied you?"

Peter shook his head slightly. "No." His eyes went to Nino, who looked uncomfortable with the conversation.

"Just so happens, Nino is writing a book on that subject. Maybe you could offer him some insight."

"Perhaps. Do you know much about that subject, Nino?" Peter asked.

"Not as much as I'd like to. Perhaps we could go into the basement later, and I'll show you what I've written so far. Your insight would undoubtedly be valuable."

"Yes. I could see how it would be."

Nino said, "In my research, I made contact with a Portland crimp named Karl Musgrove. He reluctantly agreed to give me some inside information as long as I kept his name out of the book. Have you heard of him? He apparently has a long history of that stuff."

Peter shook his head. "No. I can't say I've heard of him. I've been out of town for a while."

"Well, I received a wire this morning saying he was murdered last night. I don't know if they found the killer yet or not."

"I hope they do. It sounds like a dangerous business he was in." Peter hesitated, "He must have considered you a pretty good friend for someone to have sent you a wire."

"Well, he was helping me write the book."

Ellen asked, "Do you think he could have taken you and John?"

Peter shrugged unknowingly. "There is no way to tell. Someone forged our names on the Articles of Agreement, but I don't know who and the ship's captain wouldn't say. I had no choice but to move on and take each day as it came. I'm still trying to figure out why your mother said you lived in Oklahoma."

"She must have been mistaken. Astoria, Oklahoma, they both start and end with a vowel. She is getting older and just a mix-up in the brain, I'm guessing. Besides, she was probably as shocked to see you as I am. It's like someone we loved just rose from the dead. I still can't believe you are here."

"Me neither," Peter said softly as he looked at Nino. "How did you two meet?"

Ellen squeezed Nino's hand affectionately. "John's funeral of all places. Nino found your watch with my picture inside it and brought it to the funeral to return it to me. He thought it was John's. He wrote me a few times and we started courting several months later."

"Amazing," Peter said with a fake smile. "How did you find the watch?"

"I was a city policeman. It was in John's pocket," Nino explained.

"Wasn't John found in the river?"

"Yes. But John was found face up near the bank, and I pulled him ashore. The watch stayed dry, protecting this lady's stunning photograph. I knew the importance of such a significant heirloom and wanted to return it with my heartfelt condolences. One thing led to another and here we are. Eight years of blissful marriage and two wonderful children," Nino said with a smile before kissing Ellen.

"Hmm. It wasn't John's watch. You didn't think I was shanghaied, by chance?" Peter questioned.

"No. The investigators figured you and John were drunk and fell off a pier. It happens more often than you might think. I wasn't one of the investigators; I just happened to be called to pull John's body from the river. Other than that, I didn't know anything about you or whose watch it was. Peter, would you like to go downstairs and see what I have written for my book? If I could, maybe you'd share some of your experience with me?"

"Yes. I would like that."

Nino led the way to the basement stairs and closed the door before taking Peter into the basement. An oil lamp lit a desk. It was clear that Nino took his book seriously and worked on it every chance he could.

Nino turned a second oil lamp up, lighting the basement and then leaned against the desk to face Peter with his hands in his pockets. "Stop the BS. I know who you are and what you're doing here."

Peter nodded. "I know you do. You weren't a policeman. Your whole life is a lie. Does Ellen know that?"

"No. I've hidden my past from her, and it's going to stay that way. Her mother knows, but Grace suggested I not tell Ellen." He sighed. "Listen, I'm not the same man I used to be. I met Ellen and she changed my life. I became a Christian and confided in Grace when I wanted to confess the truth to Ellen. Grace convinced me not to because Ellen wouldn't accept it very well. You and John were both very important to her. She wouldn't understand if she knew I was responsible for what happened to you two."

"That's why Missus Whittaker lied to me?"

Nino nodded. "I know you came here to kill me like you did Karl. I won't say I don't deserve it, but I won't die easily. I won't say a word about Karl to anyone, if you will understand that I love Ellen and I love my family. We named our son after you and John if that tells you anything. I can't change the past or the way I was back then. All I can do is tell you that I'm no longer like that and care more about exposing that crime and telling people the truth and how to be safe. I'm trying to make up for my sins and make things right. I'm a Christian now and I hope, well…I hope that you will forgive me for the horrible thing I did to you."

Peter grimaced. "You think I came all this way to forgive you? Not a chance in hell! I came here to kill you for what you did to me, but now I find out you not only stole my life from me but stole my fiancée too! You're a vulture when you're not a predator. But you've made me just like you!"

"What's that supposed to mean? I'm a Christian man like you now."

Enraged, Peter snarled, "I'm no Christian! After I kill you, I'll marry Ellen like I was supposed to. Then I'm going to toss your two brats into the sea when the canoe tips over by accident or something because I will destroy you and your filthy heirs, once I marry Ellen. That's a guarantee!"

Nino sighed and spoke sincerely. "Peter, what happened to your faith? I heard you were such a strong Christian man. Where is that now? I know you went through many hard times, but the Lord protected you all this time. Do you not have any faith left?"

"What's it to you? You took everything I had away. My family, my future with Ellen, my dreams, everything!"

"It is impossible for me to take the Lord away from you; you did that yourself. You have every right to hate me, and I just wanted you to know that I'm sorry. I hoped as a Christian, you might forgive me and help me write this book together. I suppose that's too much to ask. Peter, I'll protect my family by any means necessary, but I hope I don't have to and hope you'll get right with the Lord and forgive me."

"Go to hell! I'm telling Ellen who you are. Maybe she'll divorce you on her own." He turned to walk up the stairs.

"Peter, wait," Nino said.

Peter turned around and saw Nino holding a small derringer aimed at him. "Are you trying to threaten me?"

"No." Nino pulled the trigger and placed a .32-caliber bullet in Peter's skull. Peter's body crumpled to the floor. Nino moved quickly to pull the knife from Peter's sheath and place it in Peter's hand. He stood just as the door opened and Ellen came down the stairs.

"He came at me with a knife. He was jealous, enraged," Nino explained nervously.

"I was listening through the vent, Nino. Go get the town marshal so they can get him out of here," Ellen said softly.

Her words sent waves of alarm down his spine. He lifted his eyes from Peter's body to meet her eyes. "You were listening?"

She nodded. "I already knew, Nino. My mother doesn't keep anything from me. When your friend Karl was killed, I figured Peter might come here if Karl told him about you." She pulled a single-shot derringer out of her dress pocket. "It was in case you missed or if I needed to interfere. So, I was listening. He wasn't going to leave this house alive after he threatened to murder our children. I have my family to protect, too."

"You knew what I did to him and that my meeting you was all a plan?"

Ellen nodded. "Nino, I love you. This is our family, our home, our life. I'm very thankful for it. That man," she said, pointing at Peter, "would have destroyed it and then our children. Old friend or not, his best interest wasn't in ours. He could have forgiven you, but that's not what he wanted."

"Meeting him today wasn't accidental, was it?" Nino asked.

Ellen's brow raised pointedly. "No. It was very intentional. Mary left the restaurant to tell me he was there. So, we went to the store and shopped until I saw him coming. Why do you think I told you to put a gun in your pocket? It was just in case you needed it."

"You knew what I did and stayed married to me? How could you?"

"Because I was in love with you and I still am. Now, go get the city marshal and we'll put this behind us. As a memorial to my old friend, Peter Jackson, the one I used to know anyway, you should tell his story in your book."

Bad Choices

A Wyoming Chronicles Story

W. Michael Gear

Bad Choices

THE STORMS CAME EVERY AFTERNOON, SPAWNED BY THE perpetual overcast and acrid haze that covered the Bighorn Basin. The falling sheets of rain—punctuated by strobes of lightning that knotted and throbbed like the veins in an old man's hand—left Annika Clint soaked and chilled. The cracking thunder could have split bedrock. The only upside was that the downpour had washed the faint acrid stench from the smoke-thick air. Some claimed it came from burning cities in California, Oregon, and Washington.

But then, no one had ever said the end of the world would be fun.

Most of the tortured and bruised-black clouds had drifted east beyond the peaks of the Big Horn Mountains. Water dripping from her hat and raincoat, Annika Clint shifted in the saddle. She was riding Jumper along a slick elk trail as she scouted the steep mountain slope. What they called the high pasture.

Horses have better eyesight than humans. Especially back-country horses used for hunting. Annika was cutting along just below the perimeter fence that marked the ranch boundary with the Forest Service when Jumper's ears pricked; the sorrel gelding's attention fixed on the slim figure. A woman was picking her way carefully down the rain-slick slope.

Annika reined in. Raising her binoculars, she shifted her battered old Bailey hat higher on her brow. Through the glasses, she could see that the woman was tall, wearing a smudged gray hat with a pinched crown. Her rain-damp slicker hung open to expose a fleece-lined Levi's jacket; a polished silver buckle gleamed above faded jeans. Of more interest, a rifle was balanced over the woman's shoulder. Something long, scoped. Awkward to pack.

Annika stuffed the binoculars into her coat before reaching down behind her right thigh. She pulled her battered old Sako .25-06 from the scabbard. As she did, Jumper blew, expecting her to dismount, to take a shot. Just like she would if she saw an elk. Instead she spurred him forward.

The woman had reached the elk trail, stopped, and watched Annika approach. Cupping her free hand, she called, "It's all right! I'm friendly."

Annika took another wary look up the slope—beyond the fence to the thick stands of spruce and lodgepole. Saw no one. A woman alone? Way up here?

Annika's warning bells were ringing.

"I'm Thea!" the woman called. "Thea Salva."

"What are you doing up here?" Annika shifted her grip on the Sako, balancing it over the saddle horn. A flick of her thumb would click the safety off. She had enough slack in the reins she could steady the rifle's forearm with her left as she kicked Jumper around for an off-side shot.

"Hunting. Up on the Forest Service." The woman called. Then she turned, pointing at the timber and the black storm clouds beyond. "Or I was. I was on elk. Working through the timber. I'd tied Moll, my horse, back in the clearing. I loved that mare. Bolt of lightning killed her dead."

As if to make the point, thunder seemed to roll and cascade down from the distant peaks.

"You're on Clint Ranch. Trespassing." Annika stopped Jumper twenty feet shy of the woman. Dark eyes were taking Annika's measure, the woman's face tight-lipped under a straight nose and high cheekbones. She looked to be in her thirties, fit, and athletic. Hard used.

"You Annika Clint?"

"I might be."

Thea nodded, as if fitting a piece into a puzzle. "Heard of you. People say you're a tough woman, but that you're to be relied on when things get a little Western."

"Glad to hear folks think so kindly of me. Now, what the hell are you doing wandering down into our property?"

No give in her voice, the woman replied, "Given my druthers, I'd be hip deep in a gutted elk right now. Like I said, lightning killed my mare." A pause. "Look, downhill is the fastest way to get off the mountain." She narrowed an eye as she added, "You always this hostile?"

Jumper was shifting now, fidgeting over Annika's rifle being out.

"These days? Yeah." Annika kept casting wary glances up the slope. "Wasn't bad enough that the Collapse brought the country down. Or that the government went away. Out here? Foot of the Big Horns, on a ranch? Should be the last safe place." She gave Thea a thin smile. "But we got neighbors. The kind that aren't from here. And, with no government left to speak of, they figured they'd move right in. It's come to killing."

Thea gave a half derisive snort, turning to look out across the ranch, beyond the hogbacks to the haze-obscured basin off to the west. The pastures here were lush, thick with C_3 grasses, dotted with lupine, paintbrush, and asters among the sage. And below the slope, red-sandstone hogbacks cupped green valleys. In the gap where Taylor Creek flowed, she could see Clint Ranch; the house, barn, and corrals lay astraddle the only water for miles. Call it everything a family would need to survive the end of the world.

Thea, the long rifle with its big scope still propped on her shoulder, shot Annika a probing look. "So, what are you doing way up here? Wouldn't any threat come from down below?"

"Calvin is keeping an eye on that."

"What's this trouble?"

Annika shifted her grip on the Sako. "Something you'd know about if you were from around here. And since I don't know you, maybe you'd better start talking."

Thea pursed her lips, nodded. "That's fair. I used to outfit for the Shingle Guest Ranch north of here. Up on Shell Creek. I was in Cody after the Collapse. Back when Homeland Security Director Edgewater tried to take over the Basin. The man was the legal federal authority in a time of national emergency, and maybe he did overstep his authority. No matter. Let's just say I made enemies, so a spike camp up in the Big Horns seemed like a smart thing to do."

"A spike camp?" Annika lifted an eyebrow.

"That's what people call a small camp packed into the backcountry so that—"

"Yeah, I know. But where?"

"Sylvan meadows." Thea's lips bent in a sarcastic smile. "Know the place?"

"Uh-huh." Annika squinted back up at the tree line. "But it's fifteen hard miles from here. And you did that by yourself?"

"Why not?" Thea snapped, fire in her eyes. "Like I said, I used to pack dudes into the backcountry. That's a funny question from a woman who's riding a high fence line by herself in a thunderstorm."

"So...an elk's a big critter. Even if you shot one, how were you going to gut it and pack it?"

"Honey, this ain't my first rodeo. Usually I can wrestle an elk around. Get it on its back. The trick is to cut a sharp branch to stick between the hocks, you know, keep the back legs apart. Then I split the pelvis, gut my way forward and use the pack saw to open the ribs. Get the trachea out. I've got one of those panniers that you hook over the saddle horn and cinch under the horse's belly. After that, I just butcher my way down the legs, loading the panniers. It's messy as hell. Bloody...but I get the job done."

Annika felt some of the tension leak out of her bones.

As if an afterthought, Thea added, "And you're frigging right! Fifteen *hard* miles. And packing an elk would have taken two trips with me leading Moll."

"But the lightning strike ended that, huh?"

"Which is why I opted to head down. Follow the slope to a drainage. It's Wyoming. There's always a ranch where water runs out of the mountains. And if there's a ranch, maybe I could buy, rent, borrow, or con someone into the loan of a horse. Maybe bum a saddle. Not only is mine trapped under a dead mare, but lightning's as hard on leather as it is on horses."

Annika eased the Sako back into her lap. "See anyone else? Recent tracks? Any sign that anyone's been up in the forest?"

Thea—still giving her that irritated squint—said, "Only some old horse apples where someone tied off horses in an aspen grove. Might have been a couple of months ago."

"That was us. Killed an elk up there just after the grocery in town closed." Annika nodded to herself as she shifted her Sako to a less-threatening position. Jumper must have figured out that no shooting was about to take place. The gelding relaxed to stand hipshot.

Annika tilted her head back, staring up at the roiling dark sky. "I guess if you meant us harm, you could have waited until I rode past. Shot me from ambush. The bastards damn near got Calvin that way."

"Listen, if it's a problem, I can cut south along the forest boundary. I think I hit BLM a couple of miles from here. Work my way down into the Tensleep drainage. Sounds like you got enough trouble as it is."

"Naw. It's okay. Been in a fix myself a couple of times." Annika waved at the dark sky. "Just 'cause it's the end of the world, and we're fighting for our lives, doesn't mean I have to act like an asshole." She grinned. "Might ruin my reputation for being, how did you put it? 'Reliable when things get Western.'"

A satisfied smile curled Thea's lips, and she took a deep breath that might have been relief.

"Follow me." Annika turned Jumper and let him pick his way down the slope. "Need a horse, huh? Well, hell. If there's one thing we're rich in, it's horses."

Thea matched Jumper's pace, descending the slope on light feet; the rifle bobbed where it was propped over her shoulder. "All the cow pies are old. Last year's. Height of summer? Where are your cattle?"

"Mostly run off. Or dead. Listen, it's only fair that you know. You're walking into a nasty damned fight. 'Bout two years ago, this billionaire rap artist from New Jersey called JaXX-EE-JaZZ—"

"Who?"

"Yeah, well, we'd never heard of him either. Anyhow, he decides on a wild hair that he's gonna buy up the whole west slope of the Big Horns for a wilderness retreat. Puts together about sixty thousand acres. Pays twice what the land's worth to do it."

Annika pointed off beyond the hogbacks to the distant bottoms where the Big Horn River was masked by a band of cottonwoods. "Built him a huge twenty-five thousand square foot mansion on the river. Italian marble, soaring roof, enough glass to cover a skyscraper. And, being a rich celebrity, he has a small army of security guys to ensure none of the fans, paparazzi, or curious locals can sneak in to film his pool parties and orgies."

"So, this rap singer, Jacks whats'it…"

"JaXX-EE-JaZZ. Lots of capital letters."

"Right. He's causing you problems?"

Annika shifted with Jumper as he descended a steep spot and sent rocks rolling down the slope. "Nope. So far as we know, he was at his compound in New Jersey when the shit came down. Word is the East Coast is gone. Maybe nuked. It's Gaites. Leon Gaites. The guy in charge of old JaXX-EE's security. Him and his team of New Jersey thugs. Used to be twelve. They're down to seven now. All hard cases. When the extent of the Collapse became clear, they started moving on the surrounding ranches, the ones that wouldn't sell. In exchange for political support, Edgewater turned a blind eye."

Thea skipped lightly down through a thicket of currants, barely missing a step. "I guess Clint Ranch is one of them?"

"We're like the key that opens the mountains to Gaites. We've got the only water for miles east of the Big Horn River, not to mention that our valley is the easiest access to the high country. Started out with threats. Then he cut our fences, had his guys drive off most of our cattle while we were in town. We went to drive them back. They shot at us. We shot back straighter."

"What about the sheriff? Don something?"

"Killed in an ambush along with some deputies about a month back. People suspect Gaites. No one's anxious to step into Don's shoes."

"Gaites?" Thea asked. "If he's only the security chief, even if he could force you to sell, does he have the money to buy you out?"

Annika gave the woman a cold glare. "Not to belabor a

point, but after everything's gone to hell? After Director Edgewater tried to turn the Basin into his little kingdom, what makes you think Gaites would pay even a penny for what he can just take? Look around you. It's just us. Town's a forty-five minute drive. Even if we had a sheriff, the phone's been dead for months."

Thea eased down a section of loose limestone, picking through the low-growing lupine and ground vetch. "So, if you're dead, there's no one to ask questions." She shifted the black-stocked rifle to her other shoulder. "But you said there's seven of them? How is it they haven't taken you down?"

Annika told her, "These guys came from New Jersey. Maybe they're hell when it comes to the mean streets of Newark, but they're dumber than rocks when it comes to slipping around the backcountry. Like I said, there were twelve to start with. And Sophie might have winged one the other night. The guy's flashlight was a dead giveaway."

"Sophie. Your daughter?"

"There's four of us. Me, Calvin, my son Talon, and Sophie."

"That's all that's holding your ranch?" Thea mused. "I heard somewhere that you were from Casper."

Annika reined Jumper around a couple of wind-bent limber pines and onto a game trail that angled over to Taylor Creek canyon. "Easier this way than straight down." Annika barked a bitter laugh. "Casper? Yeah. You might say I got here because of a whole string of bad choices."

"Bad choices?" Thea fell in behind Jumper, following the faint trail worn into the canyon side. "Sometimes I wonder if there are any other kind."

"My dad died when I was sixteen. Electrocuted himself while he was trying to rewire a light socket in our trailer. Mom kind of went a little crazy with the booze and pills. Lost her job. So I married the first guy to come along who acted like a tough stud. Dropped out of high school. What the hell did I know?"

Thea said, "The way you're talking, that's not Calvin, right?"

Annika pulled up at the edge of the canyon. "Take a breather. This is the last high spot. Let me take a minute to glass the approaches. From the hogback, it's seven miles across the flats to the mansion. Gaites and his guys have to cross a lot of open ground. Gives us plenty of warning."

Thea settled herself on a boulder; pulling back her slicker she extracted a CamelBak tube. The woman sucked, drinking deeply.

Point in her favor, Annika thought as she glassed the sage flats beyond the first hogback. The only thing moving out there were some cattle scattered in the raid. Seeing them out there always soured her stomach.

Lowering the glasses, Annika said, "First husband was Jess. A real piece of work. So there I was, just turned seventeen, pregnant with Talon, sleeping on a worn-out mattress on a cement floor in a crappy basement apartment, married to a drunk-and-drugged twenty-one-year-old piece of shit who'd screw anything with tits. Even when he was sober."

Thea rubbed her shins, and as she did, Annika could see the pistol and long belt knife her slicker had hidden. Well, why not? The woman had been elk hunting, after all. The only oddity would have been if she hadn't been armed to the teeth.

"How'd you get out of the basement?" Thea stood, shouldering her rifle.

Annika gave Jumper a tap with her spurs and started down the rocky trail into the canyon. "Jess didn't come home one night. The next morning he was still passed out naked in bed with some skank when the Casper police raided her place. They found enough meth to send him to the pen in

Rawlins for five years. And, being desperate and stupid, I hooked up with Woody. One of Jess's best-buddy friends."

Annika glanced back where Thea was picking her way down the steep trail, saw the woman's clamped mouth, read her disgust. Annika told her, "Oh, yeah. It was bad. Jess might have been a worthless loser, but Woody was a full-fledged son of a bitch. Into all the wrong shit with the wrong people. The violent kind. With a temper and right hook to match."

"So, you're not worth a shit when it comes to judging men? Huh?" Thea asked from behind.

"Didn't have a choice. I had a baby boy to feed. And there was generally food on the table. And it wasn't three months after Talon that I missed my period. Like, first ovulation and wham! So there I was."

"You didn't have any other family?"

Annika let Jumper pick his way to the bottom. This was well-established trail that they used to move cattle to the slope pasture. With the good footing, Annika had to hold Jumper back, Thea almost trotting behind. Granted, it was all downhill, but the woman was barely breathing hard. Maybe she was a jogger?

"Dad's family was in Denver, and I barely knew them. As to Mom's…well, they weren't the type to go to. Had a ranch outside of Douglas. Let's just say that asking for help from the 'holier than thou' would have come at too high a price."

"So…how'd you get out of Casper?" Thea finally was starting to pant as the trail wound through tall sage.

"Funny thing, that. There's a cowboy bar just outside the Casper city limits on the road to Shoshoni. Big thing. They have concerts, bands…country western hangout with a dance floor. So it's Saturday night. I'm home with the kids, and one of Woody's scarier friends shows up at the shabby apartment where we're living in North Casper. Says Woody owes him a couple thousand bucks over a car he stole, and if he don't pay by the next morrning, it's gonna be nasty. Says he'll start by having his way with me, and it won't be kind and gentle."

Annika shook her head, leading the way down the narrow bottom where the chokecherry, currants, and willow lined the trail. Taylor Creek burbled over the rocks to her left. High canyon walls, thick with trees, added to the almost claustrophobic feeling; too easy to ambush a person down here. A raven lay by the side of the trail, dead, its wings outstretched as if in desperation. They'd begun to find a lot of dead birds since the Collapse. Ants swarmed the carcass, marching in lines across the ash-coated feathers.

"I had this ratty old Chevrolet Impala, burned and leaked oil by the quart, but I grabbed up the kids and drove to the bar. It's, like, after midnight, and I locked the kids in the car at the edge of the parking lot."

"Sounds like...trouble," Thea called between puffs for breath.

"We'll stop here. Take a breather." Annika pulled up as they reached the mouth of the canyon. Jumper got his moment to nip at the thick grass that grew in the narrow floodplain. "Yep. I had to argue my way past the guy at the door 'cause I didn't have money for the cover charge. I find Woody with a bunch of his friends. Totally wasted, you know?"

"I'm starting to get the picture," Thea agreed, immediately dropping to a deadfall. She pulled out the CamelBak tube, drinking again.

Annika slouched in the saddle, staring up at the lacework of narrowleaf cottonwood branches overhead. "Band's playing, so I yell, 'Vince says you owe him two thousand bucks. Something about a car you stole! You got till tomorrow!'"

Annika laughed bitterly. "The whole table heard, and these guys, they turn, looking at Woody like he's touched a live wire. He's out of the chair like a shot. Grabs me by the arm, pulling me out of there, screaming in my ear, 'You effing bitch! You don't never humiliate me like that again!'

"And we're outside, in the dark, where Woody slaps me hard enough to bring tears, drags me over to the car. He shoves me down. Kicks the wind out of me. Pulls me up by the hair. I'm pleading, crying, saying I'm sorry. And smack, he clocks me on the side of my head. Once, twice, then I don't know how many times. My head's ringing, and I'm seeing stars and blubbering..."

Annika glances at Thea—a thunder darker than the just-passed storm behind the woman's eyes.

Annika grins. "Suddenly, it's like Woody's yanked up into the sky. The sound's like a breaking oak tree. This loud *crack*! Meaty, you know? And Woody hits the ground like boneless meat." She sniffs. "I look up. There's Calvin. Standing there, feet spread, fist knotted. This big, raw-boned cowboy in a Stetson, a snap shirt, and pointy boots. He reaches down, helps me up, and asks, 'Ma'am? You all right?'

"I'm bleeding, ears ringing, and hurting too bad to think. In the car, Talon and Sophie are bawling in terror. All I can think to say is, 'He's going to kill me and the kids.'"

"So what happened?" Thea had her wind back. The woman was in really good physical condition.

"Calvin asks, 'Can I take you someplace safe?' And I say, 'I've got nowhere to go where Woody or Vince can't find me.' Calvin gets this real serious look. 'If you don't mind helping me with a fence for a couple of weeks, I'll put you and the kids up in the bunkhouse.'"

Annika shifted in the saddle, stared at the soot rings where puddles had dried. Sometimes it did that, rained black drops from the sullen sky. She wondered what it was doing to the grass and the animals that ate it, and pulled Jumper's head up.

"Hey, I didn't even go back for my things. I just grabbed the kids out of that broke-down Chevy and piled them in the back of Calvin's crew cab. Drove half the night to get here and never left."

"Moved right in, huh?" Thea got to her feet, propping the long-barreled rifle over her shoulder.

"Took a while." Through the trees, Annika could see another black patch of clouds building overhead. Going to rain again. What had it been? Two months since they'd last glimpsed the sun? And sometimes the smoke was so low-hanging, thick, and stinking, they couldn't see past the hogbacks.

"Calvin's folks had died the winter before, and he was alone here. All he wanted from me was help stringing wire on a fence he had to build, and he was smart enough to know what a damned mess I was. He took to the kids a hell of a lot faster than he took to me. Watching that man with Talon and Sophie? I'd have sold my soul before I'd have taken them away."

"Good man, huh?" Thea asked, matching stride beside Annika's stirrup as the trail widened.

"Tough, thoughtful, kind, and caring," Annika replied. "But anyone who'd lift a hand to hurt an animal, a kid, or a woman? Cal won't abide it. Makes him crazy. He doesn't talk much about it, but I think it has something to do with his father."

"What about this ranch?" Thea asked. "How big is it?"

"A little over three thousand acres, and then there's the Forest Service lease. We ran about three hundred head. Depending on what the packers were paying, times were always thin, or sometimes even thinner. We might not have had new clothes, but we always had food on the table. I've been thankful. Especially for Talon and Sophie. The only future they would have had in Casper would have been drugs and prison. Now, every day when I look at them, I'm proud. Talon's fifteen. And a man. Sophie's thirteen, and even if I die tomorrow, she's solid. Everything I wasn't back when my dad died."

Thea glanced up from under her hat brim, a wrist draped over the rifle balanced on her shoulder. "Sounds like you've done all right."

"The only thing that scares me? I'm terrified that Gaites is finally going to figure a way to get around us. They'll just kill the men outright. Me and Sophie?" She chuckled bitterly. "If we don't die right off, given the kind of scum-suckers Gaites has working for him? Yeah, you know what they'll use us for."

"Hard to think the country's come to this." Thea was squinting out across the valley. The haze was lowering like a muggy gray curtain. Lightning flickered in the distance.

Annika shifted her grip on the Sako. "Law of the jungle. Last we heard, they were fighting down around Cheyenne. Some rumor about people swarming north out of the cities along the Front Range in Colorado."

"No rumor. Governor Agar closed the Colorado border. Used the Wyoming National Guard and militia to enforce it."

"And then that business about Edgewater? The Homeland Security director? Heard he was taking people's ranches, confiscating merchandise from stores. Word was he wanted inventories of cattle, firearms, and stuff like that. Since Gaites was between us and Edgewater, his goons never made it to our door."

"Director Edgewater was the duly appointed federal authority for the state, and it was a national emergency. He had the law behind him."

Annika rode Jumper around the thick boles of the old cottonwoods that choked the canyon mouth and into the narrow valley, bounded as it was by the hogback on the west. The trail opened up on a hay meadow; a wheel-line sprinkler system had been rolled to one side of the alfalfa field.

Thea pointed at a man's body—face down off to the right

—almost obscured by blooming alfalfa. Two ravens had been ripping at the corpse and leaving white streaks of droppings on the blood-blackened denim; they took to flight, squawking as they winged into the sullen air. "Who's that?"

"One of the twelve. Sophie shot him a little over a week ago. Just haven't had time to dig a hole and drop him in. Maybe we'll live long enough to get around to it."

Thea gave the corpse a distasteful scowl.

Annika said, "We heard Edgewater's goons were taking women. That he raided the wrong ranch over by Hot Springs, and some of their people took him and his thugs down. Blew up that mansion he confiscated up the South Fork."

"Yeah. Bad shit that day," Thea said softly as her gaze shifted from the corpse to the rich field, the alfalfa rife with blue blossoms that perfumed the air. Sounded like she was changing the subject when she asked, "Shouldn't you be cutting and baling this?"

"Can't." Annika pointed Jumper toward the ranch house, barn, and corrals where they were visible down the valley. "Like I said, there's just the four of us...and the people trying to kill us are only eight miles over to the west. Talon, Sophie, Cal, and me, we take turns on watch. Got to have eyes on the approaches to the ranch twenty-four hours a day. All it would take would be one mistake."

Thea pursed her lips, her long legs keeping pace. "You sure it's worth it? If they're killers like you say, you could just saddle up, ride out through the forest. Wouldn't that be safer for your kids? You'd get out alive."

Annika slapped a hand to her thigh. "It's like this: Calvin is fourth generation on this land. Doesn't matter that there's no law anymore. We're in the right. Gaites figured he could run us off. When that didn't work, he started shooting."

"Maybe that makes pulling out all the more reasonable."

"This is our land. We're not leaving."

Thea kept glancing back at the corpse. "What makes you think you can win?"

Annika took a deep breath. "If we can kill a couple more of them, maybe the others will wonder if it's worth it. Or, best yet, if we can tag Gaites, the others will quit. Figure they've got sixty thousand acres, what the hell do they need ours for?"

"Kind of long odds, don't you think?" Thea had an amused twist on her lips.

"It's what we've been dealt."

LOOKING out the ranch house's north window, Calvin caught sight of Annika as she rode in on Jumper. That she was accompanied by a...Yes, given the way she walked, that was a woman. But where in hell had Annika found her? And more to the point, who was she?

He climbed to his feet and clenched his jaws against the pain as he hitched his wounded leg over to the table. Now that he knew Annika was safe, he could tend his wound. Untying the binding that held the compress to the back of his upper thigh, he dropped the bloody cloth into the wash pan. Once it was soaked, he wrung out the blood into another pan. Sniffing, he thought maybe he smelled pus. That would be bad.

Standing made the wound throb. Annika had cut off the left pant leg just below his crotch to allow access to the bandage. Made him look like a fool with that one white leg ending in a fancy-stitched Lucchese riding boot with high dogger heels. And the bloody bandage could have been mistaken for a frickin' woman's garter!

He heard Jumper's whinny, answered by the horses in the corral out behind the barn. Then the sound of boots on the wooden porch. Reaching for the vodka bottle, Calvin wet the compress, positioned it over the bullet hole, and tried the strangle the gasp as he pulled the binding tight and tied it.

Damnation and hell, that hurt!

The door opened as he turned, Annika giving him a worried look. He was panting, arms braced on the table as a wave of nausea rolled through his gut.

"You all right?" Annika asked, pausing only long enough to lay her .25-06 on the table with a clunk. The woman followed, glancing back at the yard before closing the door.

"Yeah...just chipper," he said through a weary exhale.

The woman had stopped long enough to lean a long-barreled bolt-action rifle against the wall. Thing had a huge scope on it. Then she pulled her battered hat from her head and walked over with her long slicker swinging. Dang, she was taller than he, maybe by a couple of inches. But, where...?

"This is Thea Salva," Annika told him, taking his left arm. "Lightning killed her horse up in the forest. I think she's all right. Now, let me help you back to the chair before you fall over."

Calvin swallowed his grunt of agony as he braced himself on Annika and hobbled back to the chair. Each step made in brain-numbing pain.

"Looks like you caught a slug," Thea noted as she squinted down at Calvin's leg.

He puffed his relief as Annika helped him settle into the chair. His leg went from white-searing agony to a throbbing ache. "Yeah. Gaites's guys...a couple of them carry AR-15s. The rest have these stubby little semi-automatic machine gun-looking things. Like, I don't know. Uzis maybe? Nine millimeter...with big magazines. Might be good for up close security work, but worthless as tits on a boar long range. Or so I thought. Yesterday one caught me in the back of the leg." He grimaced. "Wasn't bad at first. Felt like a bee sting."

"What can I get you?" Annika asked. "Something to drink? You hungry?"

"I'm fine, darling love," he told her with a smile. To Thea, "Ms. Salva? Did Annika tell you about..."

"Yeah," Annika muttered, fretting over the binding on his leg. "All she needs is a horse. I thought she could take Smoke. He's got wind, sure-footed. And, what the hell? If Gaites ever gets the drop on us, it's one horse he won't end up with."

"I can pay," Thea said reasonably.

Annika sighed, pulled off her old Bailey hat and set it crown down on the table next to the bloody washbasin. "No, you take the horse. With the exception of more trouble than we can handle, and the chance for a real short future, we got everything we need here. But Smoke might save your life. He's packed elk, won't balk at the blood. And he's sure-footed."

Calvin added, "Ms. Salva, you got tack?"

Annika picked up the wash pan, heading to the sink where she dumped the bloody water. "Her saddle's trapped under her dead horse, and lightning-charred to boot. I thought maybe your mother's saddle?"

Calvin caught the surprised rise of Thea Salva's eyebrow as he said, "Might as well. It's the Newberry. Fifteen inch. Looks like it will fit you. Haven't waxed it lately, but it's better being used than collecting dust and going all hard in the tack room."

"Your mother's? You sure?" Thea asked hesitantly.

"She's dead, you're not. And I'd a heap rather you were riding it than leaving it for Gaites and his scum."

Thea gestured at his leg. "Bullet still in there?"

He jerked a nod.

She dropped down to a crouch, staring him in the eyes. "I can take that bullet out, debride the wound, and suture it. Call it a trade for the horse and saddle. I don't have anesthetic. You'll just have to scream. If you caught that slug yesterday, you're running out of time. You up for that?"

"How do you know how to do that?" Annika asked as she filled the wash pan at the kitchen sink.

"Guess I've spent too much time in bad places, Ms. Clint." Thea stood, looking around. "Can we put him on the table? Back of the leg? Into the quadriceps? As long as it didn't trend medial toward the femoral artery, should be a piece of cake."

That measuring stare Thea was giving Calvin unsettled him. Not that having a bare white leg in a cowboy boot wasn't humiliating enough. The damn ache was almost bad enough he didn't care. But not quite.

Calvin told her, "I don't want to cause you any—"

"You don't get that tended to, you'll end up with gangrene," Thea said. "Or dead."

"What about Gaites?" he asked. "He could hit us again at any time. Doesn't matter that it hurts, I can still shoot."

Thea shook her head. "I've seen what happens when untreated bullet wounds go bad."

Annika had crossed her arms, brow pinched with worry. "You sure you can do this?"

Something about the way Thea Salva nodded, left no doubt. "Won't be like I had a surgical kit, but I can make do. Now, there's some things I need…"

———

THE PAIN LURKED—FILLED the disjointed dreams that slowly faded from Calvin's head. The creak from the chair brought him fully awake. He lay on his stomach. In bed. Thea Salva dozed in his mother's old rocker. The tall woman's head was back, her brown hair in a ponytail. In the glow of the bedside light, he could make out faint scars on her right cheekbone and jaw.

He shifted, grunted at the sudden stab in the back of his left leg as the muscle contracted.

It might have been an electrical shock given the way Thea jumped. Instinctively, she'd reached for the pistol at her hip, fingers wrapping around the grip—a short-barreled .44 magnum given the holster and cartridges in the beltloops.

"Sorry, to wake you," he rasped. "What time is it?"

"Little after midnight." She stretched, stood, and bent over the bed to inspect his wound. Gently lifted the bandage and said, "Good. No bleeding. Don't see inflammation around the sutures."

"Where'd you learn to use a Phillips screwdriver for a bullet probe?" Calvin asked.

"Same place I learned to use a twist of number twelve fencing wire for a hemostat." A pause. "On YouTube, of course."

"Of course," he said through an exhale. "Leg still hurts. Maybe a five on a one-to-ten scale."

"Better?"

"Yep. Not as bad as times I've been bucked off in the rocks. Or when I broke my ribs. Or the time a bull trampled the crap out of me. Or when I got kicked by the old red mule. Or when I fell off the haystack. Or—"

"You're a tough man, Calvin. You didn't so much as whimper when I was fishing for that bullet."

"Ranch kid, Ms. Salva."

"Call me Thea. Need to pee?"

"No."

"Then you're not drinking enough." From beside the bed, she produced what he recognized as a CamelBak water bag and offered him the tube. "More," she ordered when he would have quit.

Satisfied she placed it back on the floor.

"Where's Annika?"

"Up on the ridge in the lookout." Thea lowered herself

into the rocker. "Sophie and Talon are both in bed. They checked in on you at sunset. Sophie kissed you on the forehead, but you were still out. Talon? He just patted your hand." She glanced absently at her rifle where it was propped beside the bedroom door. "You could have done a lot worse than those kids."

"Yep." He tried to shift, thought better of it when pain stabbed through his leg. "Breaks my damned heart that they're in this fix. The only thing they should be worrying about are grades and if their 4-H projects are going to place at state fair. Instead, they're in a shooting war."

"I've seen kids in worse," she said absently.

"Where?"

"Afghanistan. I was there at the pull out. My team was on one of the last flights out of Bagram. Remember the pictures of people falling off the airplanes? It was a hell of a lot worse on the ground."

"Military?"

She nodded. "You'd call it Special Forces work. In some missions, women can provide access, gain confidence, mislead, interrogate, get into places men can't."

"How'd you get here?"

She chuckled to herself, gaze going distant. "A long string of bad choices. After Afghanistan, I didn't re-up. Went to work for...well, we'll just call them military contractors. Volunteered for an op in Syria. We were working with some pretty rough characters and doing things the US didn't want to be associated with. It paid well, was exciting as hell." She paused. "Until an op went sideways, and a lot of people died who weren't supposed to."

For a time she sat, rocking, staring into the past.

"I guess you could say I was out of sorts for a while after that. Kind of crazy. Made some really bad decisions. The kind that carved out my guts and left my soul bleeding and numb."

Her expression pinched, and she went silent.

Calvin finally said, "You don't look like a lady with no guts. Not to me."

A wistful smile died on her lips, the gaze still empty. "Putin invaded Ukraine. Like a rope to a drowning woman, I grabbed it. Killing Russians? Now there, finally, was a chance for redemption."

"Killing Russians?" he asked softly.

"I had skills. A résumé. It was chaos at first. Stopping the Russians outside Kyiv. Then I met Tvorchi. He was a sniper. I'd had some training. He needed a spotter. Call it a match made in heaven. We both had our demons. Mine in Afghanistan and Syria, his in Bucha, Melitopol, and Kherson where his wife died and his children were sent to Russia as" —she crooked her fingers in quotation—"'orphans.' I ran on hate; he was powered by rage."

The smile that bent her lips was scary.

"I'll go out on a limb and say you were more than partners," Calvin said softly.

"Yeah," her smile widened. "Sex in the middle of a shelling? Energizing as hell."

"What happened?"

"Bakhmut." Her gaze went vacant again. "Sam and I...I started calling Tvorchi Sam. We didn't use real names for security reasons, and when he'd spot an Orc—that's what we called Russians—he'd say, 'Play it.' Like in *Casablanca*, you know?" A pause. "Then the shot. And we'd scan for another target. They just kept throwing those poor bastards at us. Sometimes our biggest worry was keeping the guns fed. The body count. Shit, we lost track somewhere past two hundred.

"We had this tradition. We'd polish our cartridge cases until they were bright. After each kill, we'd leave the empty case standing. One time, we had this hide in the ruins of the Palace of Culture on Artema Street. We lined up the cases on a board. When we pulled out, there were seventy-eight. All shining and standing in a row." Her voice had trailed off.

"And Sam?"

"My fault. Russian lines were collapsing. One night we'd wormed close to gather intel. Sam heard the Russians talking about the general. He was coming to take charge. Stop the rout." She took a deep breath. "I made the call to infiltrate their lines. Wasn't hard. Those poor bastards were just cowering in the rubble. We slithered in like snakes, found a hide in a blasted building. Could see their forward command post. Four hundred and thirty meters. Clear shot."

Her brow pinched, tension in the set of her mouth. "Next day, about noon, the Orcs really started to stir. And here he came. Colonel General Sergei Rizhmatov.

Sam said, "'Got movement. Patrol sixty meters to our left in the old bakery.' But I ignored him. I had Rizhmatov in the crosshairs, scope dialed. And I took the shot." A pause. "Gave away our position."

"They caught you?"

Thea shook her head, eyes fixed on the past. "I was in the lead, headed back toward our lines. All hell was breaking loose behind us. Shouts, gun shots. I ducked into a half-collapsed garage, scooted to the far side. When I looked back for Sam, I could see him. Atop a pile of rubble. He yells, 'I got this! Run!' Standing there, he opened up with his Kalashnikov, screaming, firing."

She swallowed hard. "And they shot him to pieces."

"But you got away?"

"Should have stayed. Fought it out. But I've never made good choices. So I exfiltrated. Never could make myself claim the kill on Rizhmatov. Couple of months after that, I quit. Couldn't take it."

"How'd you get here?"

Thea stretched her long legs, yawned again. "The only time in my life that I was happy was horse packing. Thought maybe if I could be a wilderness guide again, I could forget. So I applied for a job with the Shingle. They were full up, but the Rusty Spur Guest Ranch hired me on as a packer for the season. Then, bam. The Collapse hits. No guests are coming."

"So you hung out in the forest?" Calvin nerved himself, gritted his teeth, and shifted to ease a cramp in his good leg.

"That would have been smart, and I don't do smart. No, I signed up with Edgewater. Thought, like Ukraine, that I'd fight on the side of law and order in the face of societal meltdown." Her laughter sounded bitter. "Guess we all know where that ended up. And, you know what, Calvin? In the end, I didn't care. I'd lost so much of myself, I was just another hired gun. Like some fucking robot. Following orders. Living the good life in my off hours."

"What about that fight up at Clark Ranch? You in on that?"

"I was down on the road. That's what spotters do. Put us out front to observe. No, the fighting, the explosion, all that was up canyon. But it sure as hell put me out of a job. Then Governor Agar tries and executes Edgewater? Kind of left me high and dry with a need to be far away from Cody." She paused. "But I've always had a skill…and that's what took me to the forest above your ranch. I've always been a hunter."

He glanced at the rifle. "Looks way too long and awkward to be an elk rifle."

"It's a Gunwerks long-distance rig chambered in 7mm PRC mounting a chunk of 5x35 Nightforce glass on top." Thea lifted a hand. "I know. It's not the optimum elk-hunting rig for sneaking around in the black timber. It's about as graceful as a shovel when it comes to tight places. But, like using a screwdriver for a bullet probe and wire for a hemostat, sometimes you've got to use what you've got."

"Yeah, I guess you do."

They sat in amiable silence for a time, Calvin hating the throbbing ache in his leg. Damn it, if he could just roll over.

"What's next?" he asked.

"Riding out in the morning," she told him, that absent look in her eyes again. "You sure I can't pay you for the horse and saddle?"

"Nope. You're a good person, Thea Salva. Not enough of those around these days, so it's a pleasure to be of help when you're in need...and you need to be as far from here as you can get. After all you've been through, there's no sense in getting yourself shot on our account."

"Yeah," she said wistfully. "A good person." And then she shook her head, closed her eyes, and would talk no more.

―――――

SOMETHING WAS TERRIBLY WRONG. As morning lightened from dark to a gray overcast haze, Annika rode warily down the hogback trail, cut across the hayfield. The smoke smell and stink seemed stronger this morning.

Depressing.

She let Jumper drink before crossing Taylor Creek. Where the hell were the kids? Talon should have been up to relieve her right at dawn. Each passing second they were overdue, her fear built. As it was, she'd forced herself to wait until full sunup to give the flats leading down to the Big Horn River bottoms a final scan with her field glasses.

Had Calvin taken a turn? Was that it? Damn! He couldn't have died in the middle of the night, could he?

Heart in her throat, she glassed the ranch. Saw nothing out of the ordinary except for Smoke. The big gray horse was saddled, tied off at the corral gate. But no sign of Thea or the kids.

Pulling her .25-06, Annika let Jumper trot back to the barn. Usually she held him back. Wasn't good to let a horse head for home like that. Today—that feeling of dread like lead in her heart—she didn't care.

Riding into the ranch yard, she pulled Jumper up, looking carefully around. Nothing seemed out of order. The only oddity was the Polaris side-by-side with its dump box that they used for fixing fence. Someone had pulled it out of the shop and left it beside the barn door. Why? The thing only had a couple of gallons of gas left in it.

"Talon? Sophie?"

"They're in here, Annika!" Thea's voice came from the barn. "You'd better come see. Something tells me this will be the end of all your problems."

Annika frowned, dropped the reins, and stepped off Jumper. Her thumb on the safety, she carefully walked up to the barn door, peered in. Could see Zigzag, Sophie's horse, saddled, while Soap, Talon's gelding, was only haltered.

"Where are you?"

With a weary exhale, Thea's voice called, "Oh, for the love of mud, Annika, stop being so suspicious. Everything's fine."

Annika took a step inside, peering around. That's when she saw Sophie and Talon, both securely tied, tape over their mouths, bandanas tied like blindfolds around their heads.

"Now," Thea said reasonably, "lay that rifle down and raise your hands. If you don't, you, or the kids, are going to end badly."

Heart hammering, Annika lowered her Sako and stared in disbelief as Thea Salva stepped out from behind the tack room door, a large-caliber short-barreled revolver in her right hand.

"Sorry, Annika," Thea said, walking up and pulling the pistol out of Annika's belt. "Now, down on your knees, and cross your legs. That's it. Now, hands behind your back."

"Why are you doing this?"

Thea, voice deadpan, said, "Just doing a job."

"We trusted you."

"Yeah. Another in your string of bad choices, huh?"

———

THEA SALVA and Smoke got along great. He wasn't going to be the fastest horse she'd ever ridden. She wouldn't call him lazy, just curious to see what he could get away with. But once moving, Smoke had that feel like he could go for miles, strong, and definitely sure-footed as he climbed the hogback trail. Topping the rim, Thea pulled him up, stared back at the Clint Ranch. The buildings, corrals, and green hayfields looked somehow pristine despite the forever-brooding skies. Lightning flashed off to the south where a storm built over Worland.

From her slicker pocket, Thea extracted a walkie-talkie and thumbed the send. "Gaites? You there?"

It took three tries before her radio, with a background of static, announced, *"Thea? That you?"*

"Roger that. Job's done. Everything's tied up. If I were you, I'd load up my guys and beat feet. The place is yours."

"How'd you do it?"

"Damn fools trusted me. Bought my story about being left on foot up in the Big Horns. Made me feel right at home."

"And the kids?"

"Why would they have been a problem? World's full of kids."

"Edgewater always said you were cold and calculating when it came to getting the job done."

"Giving a damn just leads to a broken heart. Now, you got my money?"

"Ten thousand in cash. Just like I promised."

"Bring it with you."

"We're on the way. See you in fifteen!"

———

LEON THOMAS GAITES had been many things in his life, and more than once, he'd stumbled into uncommonly good luck. Not that he'd always recognized that fact in the beginning. When JaXX-EE-JaZZ had selected Gaites as detail leader for his ranch security, Gaites—born and raised in Newark— had thought the rapper had exiled him to hell.

Until the Collapse.

Rumor was that everyone on the East Coast was dead. All the cities burned to ash.

And Gaites was not only alive but building an empire.

He reclined in the passenger seat as Marko drove the big black Suburban into the Clint Ranch yard. Today, it felt really good to be Leon Gaites. Life at the end of the world had a lot going for it. Edgewater might have been taken out by the local yokels over in Cody, but if Gaites played his game smart, who knew? He might be able to step into the role as the Big Horn Basin's kingpin.

Marko stopped in front of the house, shifted the Suburban into park and killed the ignition.

Gaites chuckled to himself, opened the door, and stepped out. The only thing that would have made the day better would be if the sun had been shining. But, word was, that might take months, even years for the smoke to clear. Slamming the door behind him, he watched as Jenkin's fancy Tahoe pulled in behind the Suburban, the rest of the team piling out. HK MP5s in hand, his six guys began to clear the property.

The walkie-talkie crackled, and Gaites pulled it from his jacket pocket. "Yeah?"

"Got my money?"

"As soon as the team secures the place."

It didn't take more than five minutes. Marko stepped out of the house, calling, "House is clear, boss."

"Clear!" Sven called as his team finished their sweep of the barn, shop, and sheds.

"Where's my money?" came from the walkie-talkie.

Gaites reached for the rear door. Under his breath, he muttered, "Yeah, you heartless bitch. I hear you." But hiring her had been a good choice. And there was a ton more cash in the safe back at the mansion.

He reached out the small toiletry bag, a glitzy Armani piece. But then JaXX-EE-JaZZ always bought the most expensive thing he could find.

Gaites pulled out the walkie-talkie. Thumbed the button. "Got it right here. Pleasure doing business with you." He held it up, turning, curious about where she'd step out from.

The bullet hit him full in the sternum. Punched through him like a battering ram.

He never heard the shots that followed as his team was picked off, one by one. Was stone dead when the big gray horse was ridden into the yard, and the tall woman stepped off only long enough to pick up the fancy Armani bag.

———

"Up here!" Talon called. He stood atop the hogback, Sophie at his side where she stared pensively down at the ground, wind flipping her ash-blond hair. They waited up on the rimrock, not more than twenty yards up from where Calvin and Annika hitched their way, step by step, up the steep trail.

They didn't look like kids, Calvin thought. But then—with Calvin's leg out of order—Talon had run the backhoe. Dug the grave where they'd dumped the bodies—including the one Sophie had shot dead in the alfalfa field. No one could be called a kid after what they had been through.

"Take a breather," Annika told him, keeping a tight grip on Calvin's arm lest he stumble.

He pointed. "It's like you can see it all unfold. There's the aspen grove where Thea left us hidden in the side-by-side.

From here she could keep an eye on us. And that's where the Orcs drove into the ranch yard."

"Orcs?"

He gave her a wink. "Thea's term. And I guess she knew we'd figure a way out of those zip ties eventually."

"You up for the last little bit?" Annika asked.

Calvin turned his attention to the trail. One step at a time. Right foot first, then bring his left up. Took him nigh on ten minutes to make it, his breath puffing like a steam engine.

He thankfully stopped at the top, gasping for air. Hating the ache in his healing leg. But, damn it, last thing he'd do was laze about the ranch house. And he'd really wanted to see this.

Sophie pointed. "Right here, Dad. They're just like I found 'em."

Calvin nodded, all the pieces falling in place.

He didn't need to pick one up to know what the head stamp read: 7mm PRC. Seven of them, polished to a mirror-like gleam, standing upright on the weathered sandstone.

You May Also Enjoy:
Rebel Hearts Anthology

From the last stand at the Alamo to the events of today, it's apparent that even the most notorious of rebels are capable of love...

It's been said that the love of a woman can make the man. But what if that man is a rebel—an outlaw? When love is on the line, can a desperado truly change and be the man that every good woman wants and needs?

Six best-selling and award-winning authors have tackled this challenge.

Join along as romantics everywhere dive into this whirlwind anthology in search of an answer to the question plaguing their hearts...

What will it take for a rebel to change his ways?

The *Rebel Hearts Anthology* features sweet romance short stories by:

New York Times Best-Selling Author Kat Martin

New York Times Best-Selling Author Kathleen Gear

New York Times Best-Selling Author Sharon Sala

USA Today Best-Selling Author Kit Morgan

Award-Winning Author C.K.Crigger

International Best-Selling Author Jenna Hendricks

AVAILABLE NOW

About Peter Brandvold

Peter Brandvold grew up in the great state of North Dakota in the 1960's and '70s, when television westerns were as popular as shows about hoarders and shark tanks are now, and western paperbacks were as popular as *Game of Thrones*.

Brandvold watched every western series on television at the time. He grew up riding horses and herding cows on the farms of his grandfather and many friends who owned livestock.

Brandvold's imagination has always lived and will always live in the West. He is the author of over a hundred lightning-fast action westerns under his own name and his pen name, Frank Leslie.

About B.N. Rundell

Born and raised in Colorado into a family of ranchers and cowboys, B.N. Rundell is the youngest of seven sons. Juggling bull riding, skiing, and high school, graduation was a launching pad for a hitch in the Army Paratroopers. After the army, he finished his college education in Springfield, MO, and together with his wife and growing family, entered the ministry as a Baptist preacher.

Together, B.N. and Dawn raised four girls that are now married and have made them proud grandparents. With many years as a successful pastor and educator, he retired from the ministry and followed in the footsteps of his entrepreneurial father and started a successful insurance agency, which is now in the hands of his trusted nephew.

He has also been a successful audiobook narrator and has recorded many books for several award-winning authors. Now realizing his life-long dream, B.N. has turned his efforts to writing a variety of books—from children's picture books and young adult adventure books, to the historical fiction and western genres, which are his first loves.

About L.J. Martin

L. J. Martin is the author of 40 western, historical, mystery, and thriller novels from Bantam, Pinnacle, Avon, and Wolfpack Publishing, and of five non-fiction works. Most of his books have been produced in audio. He has a dozen books under option to film companies here and in Germany, and, as a screenwriter, has had three screenplays optioned.

He lives in Montana with his wife, Kat, the New York Times best-selling author of over 65 romantic suspense and historical romance novels internationally published in a dozen languages and more than two dozen countries. When not writing, L. J.'s working with his horses, hunting, fishing, cooking, and wandering the back country with his cameras, both video and still. His photography has appeared on national magazine covers and in periodicals.

He's particularly proud of the several hundred covers he's designed for Wolfpack Publishing, a company he helped found.

Having been car and plane wrecked, having visited (forced visits) a number of jusgados—he once threatened to write Five Star Jails of California–and one road camp, having sailed his own ketch up and down California, having raised four sons, and having been in a dozen businesses and in and out of lots of boardrooms of some of the country's largest banks, attorneys offices, and corporations, he knows about what he writes about.

About John D. Nesbitt

John D. Nesbitt bases his writing on his familiarity with the people, landscape, and animals he has come to know in the American West. He has pursued the western way of life since he first wore a black Stetson in his childhood. For the past thirty-some years John has lived in the plains country of eastern Wyoming, where he enjoys camping, hiking, horseback riding, and hunting.

As an author of more than forty books, Nesbitt also dedicates a great deal of time to reading, writing, and language study. Nesbitt writes contemporary, retro, mystery, and traditional western fiction, as well as nonfiction, poetry, and song lyrics.

His work is most often praised for its characterization, its sense of place, its prose style, and its blend of both popular and literary styles.

Readers enjoy his work because he writes about everyday people who meet challenges and solve problems in realistic ways.

John has won wide recognition for his work.

About Chris Mullen

Chris Mullen is an accomplished and award-winning author, recognized for his captivating storytelling and literary talent. Hailing from Richmond, Texas, he is a proud graduate of Texas A&M University.

With a career spanning twenty-three years in education, Chris has been a dedicated teacher in both Kindergarten and PreK, cultivating his passion for storytelling and nurturing young minds. In 2019, he received the prestigious Connie Wootton Excellence in Teaching Award—a testament to his commitment to education and his profound impact on students' lives, bestowed upon him by the Southwest Association of Episcopal Schools (SAES). It was during this time that the idea for his young adult western adventure series, Rowdy, was born.

When he's not weaving stories, you can find Chris honing his craft in local coffee shops, pizza places, or even the neighborhood grocery store. Currently, he is hard at work on an adult, contemporary western mystery series for Wolfpack Publishing.

To connect with Chris, visit his website www.chrismullenwrites.com, where you can access updates, behind-the-scenes glimpses, and much more. Additionally, be sure to follow his Amazon Author Page and catch him on various social media platforms—Facebook, Instagram, Threads, and TikTok @chrismullenwrites, as well as on Twitter @cmullenwrites. For any inquiries or heartfelt messages, feel free to reach out directly at chrismullenwrites@gmail.com.

About Ken Pratt

Ken Pratt and his wife, Cathy, have been married for 22 years and are blessed with five children and six grandchildren. They live on the Oregon Coast where they are currently raising the youngest of their children.

Ken grew up in the small farming community of Dayton, Oregon, where he worked to make a living. But his true passion always lay with writing.

Having a busy family, the only "free" time Ken has to write is late at night—getting no more than five hours of sleep every day. He has penned several novels that are being published, along with several children's stories.

About W. Micheal Gear

W. Michael Gear is a *New York Times, USA Today,* and international best-selling author of sixty novels. With close to eighteen million copies of his books in print worldwide, his work has been translated into twenty-nine languages.

Gear has been inducted into the Western Writers Hall of Fame and the Colorado Authors' Hall of Fame—as well as won the Owen Wister Award, the Golden Spur Award, and the International Book Award for both Science Fiction and Action Suspense Fiction. He is also the recipient of the Frank Waters Award for lifetime contributions to Western writing.

Gear's work, inspired by anthropology and archaeology, is multilayered and has been called compelling, insidiously realistic, and masterful. Currently, he lives in northwestern Wyoming with his award-winning wife and co-author, Kathleen O'Neal Gear, and a charming sheltie named, Jake.